THE ORIGINAL FACE

The Original Face

GUILLAUME MORISSETTE

ESPLANADE BOOKS

THE FICTION IMPRINT AT VÉHICULE PRESS

ESPLANADE BOOKS IS THE FICTION IMPRINT AT VÉHICULE PRESS

Published with the generous assistance of the Canada Council for the Arts, the Canada Book Fund of the Department of Canadian Heritage, and the Société de développement des entreprises culturelles du Québec (SODEC).

Funded by the Government of Canada
Financé par le gouvernement du Canada |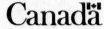

This novel is a work of fiction. Any resemblance to people or events is coincidental and unintended by the author.

Esplanade Books editor : Dimitri Nasrallah
Cover design: David Drummond
Photo of author: Virginie Gosselin
Typeset in Filosofia and Minion by Simon Garamond
Printed by Marquis Printing Inc.

LIBRARY AND ARCHIVES CANADA CATALOGUING IN PUBLICATION

Morissette, Guillaume, author
The original face / Guillaume Morissette.

Issued in print and electronic formats.
ISBN 978-1-55065-478-3 (softcover).– ISBN 978-1-55065-486-8 (EPUB)6

I. Title.

PS8626.07498075 2017   C813'.6   C2017-903130-9
C2017-903131-7

Published by Véhicule Press, Montréal, Québec, Canada
vehiculepress.com

Distribution in Canada by LitDistCo
www.litdistco.ca

Distribution in the U.S. by Independent Publishers Group
www.ipgbook.com

Printed in Canada on FSC certified paper.

"Attention is what creates value. The question is:
Is the act of getting attention a sufficient act for an artist?
Or is that in fact the job description?"
—BRIAN ENO, *A Year with Swollen Appendices*

"In art, there is no progress, only fluctuations
of intensity."
—ROBERT HUGHES

"Just endure the time of trial, and get away from
your mind of darkness."
—*FINAL FANTASY II* (USA)

ACKNOWLEDGEMENTS

Shout-out and thank you to Jessica Bebenek, Jay Ritchie, Julie Mannell, Arielle Gavin, Stephen Thomas, Sofia Banzhaf, Ashley Opheim, Teo Zamudio, Lucy K. Shaw, Oscar d'Artois, Brad Casey, Chelsea Hodson, Fawn Parker, Nicole Ruggiero, Daniel Grenier, Osamu Dazai, Dimitri Nasrallah, Simon Dardick, the app SelfControl for Mac and the Canada Council for the Arts.

CHAPTER ONE

Flaking

"I don't think I've ever wanted inner peace," I typed to Eloise on Facebook Chat. "Inner warfare just seems so much better."

Waiting for her response, I drank green tea from a paper cup. I didn't feel good or bad, but neither, like a tree. It was June something, twenty-ten-something, and I was sitting alone at a round table near a window inside one of Montreal's many Starbucks. It was hot and sunny outside. The air-conditioned Starbucks, in comparison, seemed weatherless, like a kind of non-season. Near me, a teenager was playing a space combat video game about explosions being beautiful, and on the wall in front of me was a banal painting of a red fish. "Who painted this?" I thought, abstractly focusing on the eye and the mouth. "Salvador Dali," I thought. "Just kidding," I thought.

The future, as usual, seemed dark. I was a "freelance web designer," which sounded okay, but essentially meant "70% unemployed." I was also a "new media artist" making conceptual videos that I shared online or presented at exhibits, which was only vaguely getting me anywhere. I had spent the past few months feeling deeply uninspired, unable to come up with anything, not even a simple tweet, just passively staring at my computer screen like it was some sort of hypnotic lawn ornament.

Trying to create art videos was now a source of anxiety, as opposed to an outlet for it.

Because of this, procrastinating on my own work by aimlessly browsing the internet felt more calming than usual, like a meditation retreat. I wasn't sure where all my usual creative thoughts had gone, if they had escaped my skull like feral animals into the night and were now somewhere else in the world, moving around in packs, rampaging in suburban yards maybe, or if I had just exhausted every possible thought I could have as this person, in this environment.

"Creative dry spell," I thought.

"Same," typed Eloise on Facebook Chat after a long absence. "Sorry I've been unresponsive. I just got absorbed in replying to this email."

"It's okay," I typed. "How's Baltimore?"

02

My dream job was not having a job.

03

Strategically late by about an hour, I met up with Grace and her friends at a "modern" Mexican-themed restaurant. It was a week later and Ashlyn's birthday. She was turning 25, was wearing a white knee-length dress decorated with random splashes of colours, as if fireworks had exploded on it. Next to Ashlyn was her boyfriend, Roberto. I felt relieved that Roberto was present, as he usually functioned as my default "guy friend" within Grace's friend group. "Mexican boyfriend," I thought. "Mexican restaurant," I thought. I couldn't tell if these two items were connected or not.

I removed my backpack and jacket, which was wet from the rain and glistening a little. I wanted to sit at the end of the table, next to Grace and her friend Andrea, but before I could locate a chair, Ashlyn's mom, Diane, who was visiting from Newfoundland, and who I had never met, got up and gestured to indicate that she wanted a hug, probably because I was one of Ashlyn's friends. "It's my mom," said Ashlyn, laughing. Hugging

Diane, I became overly aware that I hadn't really been around people in almost three days, hadn't even felt once, in that period, the need to socialize with other human beings.

I hugged Ashlyn's mom as a way of forcing myself to get into a social mood and Diane said, "Oh, he's a hugger," and I replied, "I am a hugger." Then Diane returned to her seat and we weren't talking anymore and didn't interact again for the rest of the evening.

I stole a chair from another table, sat next to Grace and began communicating with her in short sentences, something that felt less like a conversation and more like exchanging Morse Code by telegraph. Simply being in a stable, healthy relationship with Grace felt like a major life achievement for me, something I should win a Nobel Prize for maybe. Sitting at the other end of the table, Grace's friend, Val, smiled at me and waved a little and I waved back. Grace's friend group was composed of people she had grown up with and who had moved to Montreal around the same time as her. The group had been carefully assembled and optimized over a number of years, was sometimes pruned like a bonsai tree to maintain the desired shape. This was very different from my approach to friendship, as my friends rarely came together as a single group. They all had, at one point or another, landed individually in my life, like lost Frisbees, and would probably exit it in the future, to be replaced by new individual, single-usage friends.

One major difference between Grace and me was that I didn't expect my friendships to be permanent.

Grace asked me if I was planning on ordering anything and I replied that I wasn't sure I wanted to spend money. She introduced me to a friend of Roberto's, Jorge, who was visiting Canada for the first time. Jorge seemed amused by Montreal, observing people around the table like he was watching a play about the social customs of young adults in Canada. I glanced at Andrea, who was staring at her phone and touching the screen with her finger, as if tickling it. I needed a new artist photo for my website and wanted to ask Andrea, a freelance food photographer who also worked part-time in a print shop, for help, but couldn't get myself to. I still felt shy and asocial and ostrich-like, mostly unable to process human interactions. I imagined myself, a grown man, being banished from the adults' table due to inadequate social skills, ordered to go sit at the children's table instead.

I felt grateful that there was no children's table in the restaurant.

Overhearing Ashlyn's laughter, I thought about how she was turning 25. I visualized myself at age 25, a period of my life that now felt both distant and near, like an illusion of false perspective. I placed my head on Grace's arm and said, "Hug my head," in a soft voice and she did, covering it with her other arm and squeezing gently. Grace said, "Why your head?" and I replied, "It's where all the good things happen," without thinking and then we both laughed a little. A waitress carrying several items approached the table. Grace and Andrea's order was a shared plate of tacos stuffed with black beans. Before the waitress disappeared again, Andrea ordered a daiquiri. Grace drank water from her glass, emptying it and then tactically refilling it from a bottle of Bacardi hidden in her handbag.

"You can have some if you want," said Grace.

"Thank you," I said. "Sneaking in drinks is so much more fun than buying them."

"I know," said Grace, prolonging the last syllable.

"We're totally out-partying that other table," I said, pointing at a group of seven seated at a table across the room. From my point of view, they seemed less like human beings, and more like well-operated puppets.

"When we got here, I thought they were us," said Grace. "I thought the open wall was our reflection in a mirror for some reason. They kind of look like us. It didn't seem like we were having fun."

"They look really bored," said Andrea. "Maybe it's no one's birthday for them. Maybe it's just a Wednesday."

"They look like they're from an alternate universe where we all have jobs," I said, taking a sip from Grace's glass.

"I have a job," said Andrea.

"Real jobs," said Grace, laughing a little.

The waitress returned with Andrea's daiquiri, prompting Grace to hide her drink. Andrea's beverage was red-colored and looked planet-like in texture and composition. I stared at the drink absent-mindedly and thought, "Morgan Freeman," and then, "Morgan Freeman narrating a space documentary about this daiquiri." Using her phone, Andrea filmed her drink for a few seconds, zooming in and out overzealously, then sent the recording to someone through Snapchat.

I continued to drink Bacardi with Grace, began to feel, several sips later, more or less normalized, the alcohol calcifying a false sense of confidence, making me officially cede command of my body to my social persona. I mentioned the website photo to Andrea, who automatically agreed to help, even offering to do it for free. We began discussing when to meet, but were interrupted by the waitress surprising Ashlyn with a chocolate lava cake. Many people used their phones to photograph Ashlyn and her birthday cake.

"I wish the camera on my phone wasn't broken," said Grace. "I miss Instagram."

"I don't know," I said. "I think we're okay. I feel like this moment is being over-documented right now."

"I know I'll be able to look at everyone's photos later, it's just," said Grace, "it's not the same."

About half an hour later, we exited the Mexican restaurant and walked in unplanned groups of three or four to Sharx, a bar located a few streets down that contained a bowling alley. Unbothered by the rain, I sprinted ahead to join the lead group of Ashlyn, Roberto and Derek.

"Thank you for the shirt," I said to Derek, who was Ashlyn's roommate. I didn't know him very well, but had recently, through Grace, inherited an expensive-looking shirt from him. "I actually really like it."

"Oh, my pleasure," said Derek. "I was just trying to get rid of it. I own way too many blue shirts."

"I have been broke for a while now," I said, "so this is really good for me."

"What's going on with you?" said Derek. "Grace was saying that you're thinking about moving to Toronto, but you weren't sure."

"We've talked about it," I said. "I really like Montreal, but it's starting to feel like I've done everything that I needed to do here. My friend Eloise lives in Toronto and I've already been there a few times. It seems like there would be new opportunities for me if I lived there."

"I could see why that would make sense for you," said Derek. "It's too bad if you're moving, though. I mean, I don't know you very well, but Grace really seems to like you."

"It's a lot to think about," I said.

Grace and I had originally met through my friend Jane, who knew her friend Ashlyn. We had been dating since November.

Grace was 32, three years my senior, and worked part-time as a hostess in a primarily anglophone Irish pub and grill in Monkland Village, where she only had to know a few basic sentences in French. She had short, dark black hair and walked with a very slight limp as a result of an old soccer accident. She was more extroverted than me, seemed to feel energized around people, enjoyed talking and socializing and living her life unironically. In addition to her job, she was also completing individual courses like biology and chemistry, prerequisites that would eventually allow her to apply to a physical therapy program at McGill University in Montreal, her first choice, or U of T in Toronto, her fall-back plan. Earlier in life, she had studied communications and later social work, each time dropping out before graduating. Her complicated journey towards something resembling a career meant that we were currently at similar points in our lives, and, therefore, romantically compatible.

Unlike most people around her, Grace wasn't an artist. She sometimes described herself as "boring," especially when comparing herself to her close friends, whose social media presences were all catchier, more exciting and better-liked than hers. She could play the guitar very well but rarely did, the electric model and amp in her room mostly accumulating dust. What I liked about her was simply that she was a good person, stable, kind, reliable and caring. We both tended to say "I am sorry" a lot, were always trying to out-apologize one another, as if our relationship was a kind of BDSM in which the safe word was "sorry."

Grace was also, I felt, someone whose trust and desire to trust had been abused in the past, the kind of person who could only figure out what a "healthy relationship" was by deducing from what it wasn't, like trying to determine who the culprit was in a game of Clue. Based on stories she had told me, I

17

sometimes visualized her ex-boyfriends as a kind of museum display of deranged jerks. One was a graffiti artist who, one night, had gotten too drunk and insulted her friends, then later stolen her bike. A few months before, Grace and I had run into him at a house party, resulting in an unpleasant conversation that had quickly escalated into a shouting argument. "But what's the value of someone's life compared to a cheap bike?" her ex-boyfriend had said in defense of his actions.

Judging from her agitated response, it seemed clear that, to Grace, the value of this specific person's life was worth much less than the cheap bike.

Entering Sharx, I spotted an ATM machine and decided to take out money. I wasn't sure there would be sufficient funds in my bank account for me to withdraw $20 plus processing fees, but I was able to complete the transaction without any objections from the machine.

Retrieving money from the dispenser, I felt like I had just won some sort of private lottery.

Downstairs, I ordered a beer, received Alexander Keith's in a tall glass, paid for the overpriced drink without leaving a tip. Rejoining Grace and her friends near the shoe station inside the bowling alley, I asked Roberto if he was good at bowling and he answered, "I don't remember," which made me laugh, though he hadn't intended the remark as a joke. I told Grace that I had "zero interest" in bowling and she replied, "Are you sure? I can lend you money for a game," and I said, "No, it's okay," in a calm tone.

Several minutes later, I sat on a teal couch near our group's assigned lane and observed Jorge, who seemed intrigued by the large television monitor above the shoe station. The television screen was displaying the third period of a Stanley Cup hockey game in the middle of June. The only other person in the bowling alley looking at the monitor was a random man in a trench coat who was clapping to encourage the athletes on television, though the athletes on television seemed unaffected.

Grace sat next to me and we shared my drink while holding hands. Later, after finishing the beer, I brought the empty glass with me to the men's room, where I locked myself in the only unoccupied stall. I retrieved a tall can of Sleeman hidden in my backpack, snapped it open and calmly transferred the can's content into my empty glass. I began thinking about how this situation, sneaking beers into public places to save money, was just normal behaviour for me, how this way of living, having little income and keeping my responsibilities and the overall cost of my existence to a minimum, was what I had decided was the optimal arrangement of my life in Montreal, a kind of Feng Shui gone horribly wrong.

"My comfort zone would be someone else's depressing wasteland of unemployment," I thought.

Coming back, I saw that Grace was having difficulty bowling, mainly because the ball was too gigantic for her. I glanced at the scoreboard, noticed that Roberto, despite having gutter-balled several throws, was now in the lead. Roberto looked surprised by this, but not unproud, as if impressed by his skill at this seemingly random, strategy-less game. The television monitor above the shoe station was now presenting professional wrestling, which Derek was watching, or trying to watch. On the television monitor, a wrestler with a beard was holding a microphone and arguing with a wrestler dressed in a suit and a tie.

"I wish this had subtitles," said Derek. "I love wrestling. I just never watch it."

"Why are they so angry?" I said. "They're just talking right now. Even talking is making them angry."

"Everything makes them angry," said Derek. "That's the point of wrestling. So they always have a reason to fight. You couldn't be a wrestler otherwise."

"So there's no wrestler with good conflict resolution skills?" I said.

"That would be a terrible wrestler," said Derek. "Or wait, no. People would want to see him get his ass kicked. They would make him world champion."

After the game, whose winner was apparently no one, as most players seemed uninterested in the final tally and eager to move on, I replied to a text message from Jane while Grace, Andrea and Ashlyn discussed what to do next. Andrea mentioned that she wanted to go to a loft party at which the band Blue Hawaii was either playing or DJing, she wasn't sure, but then was successfully out-lobbied by Ashlyn, who convinced everyone to relocate to a bar in the Gay Village.

Several minutes later, we all stood in the entrance at Sharx, mentally preparing to face the rain again. Half the group agreed to share a cab while the other decided to travel by subway.

"Are you coming with us?" said Grace.

"I don't have a subway thing," I said.

"How did you get downtown?" said Grace.

"I walked," I said.

"You walked?" said Grace, with an inflection that sounded like an accusation.

"It took me, like, fifty minutes," I said. "I hadn't gone out all day. It was fine. I think I'd rather walk to the Village as well."

"I can lend you money to get the night pass," said Grace. 'Then later we can take the bus to get back to my house."

"It's okay, I have money with me," I said. "I just don't want to spend it. I don't mind walking. It would take me twenty minutes to get there. I'll walk."

"But it's pouring outside," said Grace.

"It's not pouring," I said. "It's just raining."

"Let me pay for you," said Grace.

"No, it's fine," I said. "Never mind, I'll buy the night thing."

"Are you sure?" said Grace.

"Yeah, it's okay," I said. "Forget what I said. I'll just buy the night thing."

"Okay," said Grace.

I walked with Andrea, Val and Grace to the Guy-Concordia metro station in unintentional silence, the weather thwarting our attempts at conversation. Inside the station, I stopped at an automated vending machine while the rest of the group passed through the turnstiles. "Hold on, Daniel needs to get a night pass," said Grace, forcing the others to wait. Swiping the pass at the gate, I was denied access and shown the error message "Plage horaire interdite."

"What's wrong?" said Grace.

"It's telling me that I can't get in," I said. "Hold on."

I sprinted to the booth attendant, who was reading a magazine.

"Excuse me," I said in broken French. "I just bought this and it's telling me that I can't use it for this time slot."

"It's after midnight," said the attendant in French. "You need to activate the night pass before midnight. It doesn't work otherwise. It'll work tomorrow night."

"But I just bought it," I said.

"Well, I am sorry," said the attendant.

On the other side of the turnstiles, a distressed-looking

Grace began shouting things in English like, "He just bought it, I saw him," trying to help. After arguing with me a little more, the attendant offered to trade me a regular, single-usage ticket in exchange for the night pass and a small additional fee. I thought, "This is bullshit," and felt within me an unknown amount of anger sparked by poorly timed personal pride. I looked at Grace and mouthed, "I'll just walk," and she said, "Wait," and moved in my direction. She wanted to discuss this with me further, but I repeated, "I'll just walk," in a firmer tone and added, "I'll be there in twenty minutes."

I climbed the stairs and exited the station. I began walking east, tried to convince myself that leaving abruptly was the moral thing to do in this situation. "I am broke," I thought. "I really can't waste money right now. Also, I like walking. What's the difference?"

Around me, fine translucent needles were coming down from the sky in a screensaver-like manner, as if they made up a detailed pattern obeying its algorithm. I glanced ahead through the rain, saw moon-drenched buildings in the distance. The city of Montreal looked withdrawn and self-conscious, as if it was thinking, "I keep getting bigger and bigger, but I still feel like I have no idea what I am doing."

I walked on Sainte-Catherine and eventually reached the Gay Village. I located the bar, tried going in, but was stopped by a doorman. There was a cover charge, I was told. Feeling annoyed, I looked past the man to register the bar's vibe, which didn't seem particularly promising. I thought about leaving, going home. I retrieved my phone and saw that Grace had messaged me a few minutes earlier to warn me of the charge at the door. I composed a text message explaining that I didn't want to pay the mandatory fee, didn't feel like being social anymore, would be leaving. Then I thought, "Wait, I am being an asshole, I suck for wanting to go," and deleted the original message. I composed a second text asking Grace to come see me at the door.

About a minute later, I saw her getting up and walking towards the entrance. I wanted to tell her that I wasn't sure I wanted to stay, but looking at her directly, I realized that she was upset.

"Are you okay?" I said.

"I didn't want to make you waste money," said Grace, becoming emotional a little midsentence. "I am sorry I made you buy the night thing."

"Hey, it's okay," I said in a warm tone of voice. "I am not mad. I know I've been saying that I need to be careful with money, but money is stupid. We shouldn't argue about money. I am sorry I stormed out earlier. That was probably just misplaced ego on my end. It's my fault. I am dumb."

I placed her head against my chest and hugged her. I was surprised that she was crying a little, didn't think she would be over something as simple as this. Though we had been dating for five months, we hadn't, in that period, fought, not even once. On a few occasions, we had even joked about what the topic of our "first fight" would be, if it would sound something like, "Listen, I am sorry that I am upset with you, but you can't expect me not to react this way after what you did, though I apologize if me being upset makes you upset, that wasn't my intention, I just want what's best for you." In reality, I suspected that our first real fight was going to be about Toronto. I knew that if I decided to move there, I would probably become just one more disappointing man in her life, and that if she was upset, it wasn't because of money at all, but because she liked me and was afraid of losing me, didn't want to give me any reason to distance myself from her.

We kissed. I began to think that what I wanted was no longer to go home, but for her to feel good again. I grabbed her hand and paid the cover to get into a bar I didn't want to be in, with money I wasn't sure I had. We sat at a table with her friends and I began chatting with Roberto, then with Derek and Val. My mood suddenly seemed radically different, as if it had been imported from another brain, one created from scratch in an underground lab that had the ability to maintain, at all times, ideal levels of dopamine and serotonin.

I came up with little jokes.

I told a story.

I made Grace laugh.

04

I woke up at Grace's apartment, in Grace's bed and with Grace's cat, but without Grace. In my sleep, I had accidentally drooled on one of her pillows, leaving a signature that looked like a territory marker, some sort of unmotivated graffiti that didn't involve getting out of bed. I searched her nightstand for my glasses, but could only find rolling papers and a Ziploc bag that contained a small amount of weed. Locating my pants on the floor, I checked my phone for the time and saw that it was 1:30 p.m., meaning Grace had already left for work. Grace's cat, an overweight, comical-looking eight-year-old male named Tom-Tom, was monitoring my actions. His eyes were wide open and he looked overly alert, like an undercover cop.

"Grown man arrested by cat for trespassing and vandalism," I thought.

I petted Tom-Tom a little. His black fur had a peculiar tex-ture, as he wasn't very good at cleaning himself, too large to reach certain areas. Rejecting my attempt at affection, Tom-Tom jumped from the bed and ran towards the kitchen in an unintentionally funny, animated GIF-like manner. I liked Tom-Tom, liked how he existed outside of language, how he didn't have words like "comical-looking" to describe his own condition, and therefore was unaffected by them.

An hour later, at Résonance, a café at Parc and Fairmount, I replied to an email from Jane, who wanted to present some of my videos as part of an "art night" she was organizing. We wouldn't make money because she had to pay for the space, but it was "good exposure," the email said. I logged into my online bank account, transferred the last $900 in my savings account to my regular account, then tried working on things. Once again, I felt blocked, couldn't seem to produce anything. "How do I unclog my brain so that new ideas trickle in?" I thought. I wasn't sure what the spiritual equivalent of a toilet plunger was supposed to be.

For a while, I just sat there in my own irrelevance, killing a browser tab only to generate two or three new ones, like cutting the head of a hydra.

Though Résonance was usually quiet during the day, minus maybe creepy jazz playing on the sound system, that afternoon, a music teacher had reserved the concert area in the back. One by one, small children of seven to nine were summoned onstage to play a few notes on an oversized piano. At the end of each song, the children's parents clapped politely in a forced and mechanical manner, like a kind of Pavlovian conditioning in which silence automatically triggered applause. Distracted by the performance, I thought about how, for the children, this was a pretty accurate simulation of what life as an artist would be like, performing in front of a modest audience and then receiving polite clapping as a response partly because you weren't horrible, and partly because you were done.

"I am in a library stealing their Wi-Fi," typed Eloise on Facebook Chat. "I just got an overly aggressive email from someone I went to school with."

"Aggressive about what?" I typed.

"She said she doesn't like my online magazine and 'self-promotion' and that she didn't want to 'boost my ego' anymore, because I've been getting so much love from people," typed Eloise. "I said, 'I spend 95% of my time alone.'"

"That sucks," I typed.

"She also said that I hate men," typed Eloise. "I tried to tell her that I don't hate men, it's just easier to assume that they're evil by default. They can still earn my trust over time. She didn't seem to get it."

"I don't know if you should take this too personally," I typed. "It sounds like she hates your Facebook, not you."

"Yeah," typed Eloise. "I mean, I get it. I hate my Facebook too."

"How long are you staying in Baltimore again?" I typed.

"Another month," typed Eloise. "That was always the plan, get away from Toronto and stay here for two months. I like Baltimore, but it's not my life. It feels like I've borrowed this life from Julie. It's a way better life, arguably. I am Julie. Sometimes I think about moving back to Toronto and it's like, 'Why would I do that?' But then I have to exist somewhere."

"How do I move to Toronto?" I typed. "Part of me wants to, but another part of me is still sabotaging that first part's efforts. Shit-talking it a little."

"You should just move without thinking about it," typed Eloise. "Buy a one-way Megabus ticket, bring the strict minimum with you and abandon the rest of your stuff in Montreal, for future civilizations to study. That's what I did when I left for Baltimore."

"I won't be able to move until August," I typed. "I could have tried for July first, but then I waited too long."

"Are you sure this is what you want?" typed Eloise. "Toronto, I mean."

"I think so," I typed. "Every four years or so, I always end up doing something drastic to fuck up my life. It's like the Olympics of poor life planning. I would be right on schedule."

"Have you told Grace?" she typed.

"We talked about it once, but never as something that's definitely happening," I typed. "She would be disappointed if I moved. We've only been dating since last November, but I feel like it's bigger than that for her. I think her goal in life is to prove to her dad that she's not failing at life, so she wants to have a decent career and maybe get married and have babies and stuff. She's already thinking about these things."

"Wow, babies," typed Eloise. "That seems like a huge amount of pressure."

"I like Grace a lot, and we get along really well, but I have no idea how to explain to her that I hate every single human baby on a personal level," I typed.

"Lord, I don't want babies either," typed Eloise. "Life is so complicated already, why would you add children on top of that? It's like you're deliberately trying to go insane."

"Does it have to be a baby?" I typed. "Why can't we just have another adult?"

05

I often felt like some of my best friends were websites.

27

Whereas before not all my ideas were great, but at least I had some.

One of the Ten Commandments should have been, "Avoid taking yourself seriously."

After sex, I rested my head on Grace's chest, synchronizing my breathing with hers. It was 2 a.m. and several days later. We had recently stopped using condoms, as this made sex more pleasurable for us. Instead, Grace tracked her period using a period app on her phone and I pulled out at the last minute to ejaculate on her stomach. We both knew this system wasn't ideal, but were apparently using it anyway.

I asked Grace what her plans for the weekend were and she mentioned something at La Brique.

"We've been there so much lately," I said. "I feel like I am going to blow my head off if we go. I don't know if I want to make a scene."

"I want to go, but you don't have to come with me," said Grace. "You can flake."

"It just seems like we've been partying on autopilot lately," I said. "When we go out, it's always the same four-five venues and the same rotating cast of people and the same conversations. It's like being in a sitcom that has to revert to its default situation before the episode is over. I am just standing there thinking, 'I am trapped.' It's not a good feeling."

"Well, there's no point in partying if you're not having fun," said Grace.

"It's more complicated than that," I said. "It's almost like I am tired of having fun."

"What do you mean?" said Grace.

"Never mind," I said. "I don't know what I mean. I remember, when I was seeing Evil Cayla, partying with her was always unpredictable. She had this knack for getting into insane situations all the time."

"You always call her 'Evil Cayla,'" said Grace. "If we ever break up, are you going to refer to me as 'Evil Grace'?"

"No, not at all," I said. "If anything, you would be, like, 'Emotionally-repairing Grace.'"

"Emotionally-repairing Daniel," said Grace, smiling. "Do you have photos of Evil Cayla?"

"I could show you her Facebook if you want," I said.

"Please," said Grace with enthusiasm. Except for Evil Cayla, who I had shit-talked on a few occasions, Grace didn't know a lot about my dating history. My romantic life, prior to her, had felt more or less like a dying plant, something that received water and sunlight once in a while, but was never really flourishing. For that reason, it was hard for me to allow myself to love because I had difficulty believing it would last. Another major difference between Grace and me was that I didn't think having a stable romantic partner was going to solve any of my problems.

While I reached for her laptop, which was on the floor, Grace retrieved weed, rolling papers and a book from her nightstand. "Oh, good," I said, locating Cayla's profile on Facebook. "I wasn't even sure we were still friends. We probably have the record for most amount of times that we deleted and then re-added one another on Facebook."

"How many ex-girlfriends do you still have on Facebook?" said Grace.

"Not that many," I said. "I've been single a lot, so I am definitely not, like, the king of relationships."

"God, me neither," said Grace while rolling a joint, using the book as a base. I glanced at her hands and couldn't help feeling like the author photo of Pulitzer Prize-winning writer Jennifer Egan was observing her manipulate weed.

"Here, this is me and Cayla together," I said, pointing at the screen. "I was pretty drunk the night this was taken. I remember, I tried to high-five a wall."

"She doesn't look that evil," said Grace. "The way you talk about her, I kept imagining the rich lady from the *101 Dalmatians*."

"She's too evil to look evil," I said.

"She's pretty," said Grace.

"Show me one of yours," I said.

"One of my ex-boyfriends?" said Grace, emphasizing "my." "Oh God. Well, you met Michael the bike thief, we don't need to see him again. Maybe I could show you my Australian ex-boyfriend."

"You have an Australian ex-boyfriend?" I said.

"From high school," said Grace. "He was on exchange. We were never officially boyfriend and girlfriend, but out of all the guys I've been involved with, he's the only one my dad has ever liked. He still talks about him. 'How's Martin these days?' I have no idea, Dad. It's been more than ten years."

I ceded control of the MacBook to Grace. About a minute later, a photograph appeared onscreen. In the picture, a bald man with a beard and a lime green t-shirt was holding a baby while sitting in front of a tent in a forest. Grace explained that her Australian ex-boyfriend had changed a lot since high school, didn't have the bald head or the baby or the lime green t-shirt back then. We cycled through her ex-boyfriend's profile pictures, making little comments and laughing while doing so.

"Do you want to see my first serious girlfriend?" I said. "It's this French Canadian girl, we dated when I was 17 or 18. I haven't lurked her in a while, so I don't know what to expect."

Holding the MacBook again, I tracked down my French Canadian ex-girlfriend's Facebook account. In her most recent profile picture, she had blond hair and was wearing what appeared to be a cowboy hat.

"I have no idea what's going on in this photo," I said. "She's changed so much. This is honestly mind-blowing."

"That's what makes it fun," said Grace, "that she's changed."

"It's been so long," I said. "I feel like we're new people now. We could probably date again without realizing that we've dated before."

"That would be funny," said Grace. "It sounds like the plot for a movie."

"By Woody Allen," I said.

"Definitely," said Grace.

"Show me another," I said.

"Okay," said Grace. "I can show you Kevin, but please be nice. You'll see why."

I wasn't sure what Grace was afraid of, but I promised I wouldn't be mean. About a minute later, she pointed at the screen and said, "Here, this is us."

"He seems like a nice sports bro," I said. "But you look so different in this."

In the photo, Grace was about twenty or thirty pounds heavier. Her younger face looked like an unoptimized version of her current face.

"That's why I didn't want to show you," said Grace. "I untagged myself from this photo. When I moved to Montreal, I started walking more and my eating habits changed and Dad wasn't there to make me feel bad about myself anymore, so I dropped a bunch of weight without realizing. When I returned home, everyone kept telling me how great I looked, and I was like, 'What the hell are you guys talking about?'"

"Does your dad still make you feel bad?" I said.

"It's better now," said Grace. "We just couldn't live together. He means well, but he can be very OCD about certain things. He would point out blemishes on my face, make me feel bad about my weight or yell at me all the time to keep my room clean. He would tell me things like, 'No man is ever going to love you if you can't clean up after yourself.' He thought he was doing me a favour, but when you hear the same thing over and over again, you start to believe it. No man is ever going to love me."

"Do you remember the first night I slept at your place?" I said. "You were being self-conscious about your room and I was like, 'Cool, piles of clothes on the floor.'"

"The self-conscious thing, that's definitely because of my dad," said Grace. "I am pretty sure he has an undiagnosed something. Realistically, I might be undiagnosed with something too, like ADHD. That would explain all my failures in school. When I was a kid, my teachers were always telling my dad the same thing. 'Grace is a smart student, but she's good at talking and she's always handing in her assignments at the last minute.'"

"That's true," I said.

"What's true?" said Grace.

"You are good at talking," I said.

On Instagram, I saw that Eloise had posted a photo of herself wearing a t-shirt that said "I bathe in male tears."

10

So much of my art career was still imaginary.

11

I woke up in the middle of the night and Grace was saying, "I am sorry," in her sleep.

12

Looking out the front window, I could see a couple across the street micromanaging a baby. The sunset, currently peaking, had transformed into a gorgeous, unsustainable orange. It was the last day of June and I was standing in an art gallery on a particularly warm night, feeling more curious about the baby than about the art around me. I sometimes felt as if I had lost all concept of "family." As a result, the life of a parent often seemed as mysterious and inaccessible to me as the life of a nocturnal animal. I was at an age where I probably should feel social pressure to "settle down," except I didn't. I wasn't talking to my parents anymore, wasn't close to my family, and none of my friends were married or had children. All I had, instead, was the knowledge that partying had begun to feel like North Korea, a kind of elaborate deception that tried to make you believe that you were ageless. I was starting to feel like I wanted to take my life more seriously, make decisions that weren't selfish, weren't terrible, but also weren't compromises.

"A performance," I thought, observing the parents caring for the baby. I felt like I was watching an art performance, a piece titled *Avoiding Self-Centredness in a Post-Internet World Through Love, Altruism and Devotion.* "So much free wine here," said Jane, suddenly popping into my field of view like a foreign object from another dimension. "It's like I am crashing a wedding." She laughed. She was wearing a black top and a transparent blouse adorned with blue petals, had arranged her hair in two small buns, making her look, I felt, futuristic, like a calming apparition from a non-dystopian, seemingly trustworthy to-morrow. We were attending the launch of the new issue of an online art magazine, which had organized a projection of animated GIFs curated by a new media artist who was popular on the internet. The GIFs, supposedly, all dealt with how gender, sexuality and class were presented online.

"I have to say, I am little bummed that neither of us were solicited for this," Jane said.

"I know," I said, "but we can't be solicited for everything. There are so many people making things out there. Everyone has a Tumblr."

"That's too bad," said Jane.

"It's too easy to create stuff now," I said. "Maybe we would be more special if we did nothing, like if we had full-time jobs and didn't bother with social media and came home at night and felt good about ourselves. Everyone else would still be an artist, so we would stand out."

"I could see that," said Jane. "These guys are killing it! They don't give a shit about their followers! It's an ironic comment on America in the post-Facebook era!"

34

"No one ever talks about the damage that art does to your self-perception," I said. "It's like, if you put together a show and get even just a tiny bit of praise from somewhere, you start thinking things like, 'I can't work at Foot Locker, I am an Important Artist who got a tiny bit of praise from some place, what would my fans think?' From that point on, you're always an Important Artist to yourself. You always deserve better."

"I agree with you that there's too much content out there now," said Jane. "We're all suffocating. Lately I've been feeling like I am tapped into culture 24/7. It's like a burning sun. Get me away from it!"

She laughed again.

"Maybe what we need to do is create anti-content," I said. "Content that destroys other content."

"I could see that," said Jane, smiling.

She and I had been friends for a little over two years. Like me, Jane had a BA in something art-related, though didn't see the point of pursuing her studies to get her MA or MFA, which would require taking out student loans and going deeper into debt. She lived in Mile End, where she shared a studio with her boyfriend, who was a musician, and her dog, a thirteen-year-old golden retriever named Dora. Jane didn't have a full-time job, or maybe not having a job was her full-time job. She sometimes babysat for wealthy families living in Westmount, who paid her in cash, and volunteered at a yoga studio one day per week. She had also recently begun receiving social assistance from the government. For her application to go through, she had had to sit in a waiting room lit like a funeral home, wait for several hours, then cry in front of government employees on three separate occasions.

What I admired the most about Jane was her spontaneity,

positive energy and desire to be alive. Artists often turned out to be power hungry and insecure and conservative and sort of bovine overall, but Jane wasn't like that. Her art practice seemed, to me, less like a celebration of her own ego, and more like a manifestation of a genuine desire to connect with others. Her work was primarily centred on videos, live performances and installations that tackled themes like technology, the natural world, reality and the human body. When I compared Jane's art to mine, I sometimes felt like we were asking completely different questions, but searching for the same answers.

"Last night, I had this amazing experience with the boy I babysit," said Jane. "Jacob is three years old, so everything is amazing to him. Yesterday, he pointed at the sky and said, 'Look!' and I was like, 'You want to look at the moon? Hell yeah, we can look at the moon.' And I am not gonna lie, it was amazing. I don't think I'll ever make anything that's even half as cool as the moon."

"Instead of the projection tonight, maybe we should all just go outside and look at the moon together," I said.

"That's a good idea," said Jane. "We can do that at my art night. By the way, you don't have any new material we could show that I don't know about, do you?"

"Not really," I said. "I've been going insane trying to create something new that I like, but for some reason, nothing's working. I think I want to make something that's 'better' than what I've done before, except I have no idea what I mean by 'better.'"

"Don't think of it as better or worse, just go with what feels right," said Jane. "Go with what you know."

"That's the problem, I feel like I don't know anything other than my problems," I said. "I am a respected scholar in the field of my problems."

"Maybe you should smoke a bunch of weed," said Jane. "Weed always gives me clarity. Though sometimes clarity just tells me to get more weed."

"That's funny," I said, laughing.

"I should write that down," said Jane. "I've been noting down my thoughts lately."

Jane took out her phone and selected a note-taking application. A page filled with basic, sometimes nonsensical sentences appeared on screen. "Horror movie about killer ladybugs," read one sentence.

"These notes are such a mess," said Jane. "Look, it starts as different thoughts, then there's a phone number, and after that it turns into a recipe."

"What does this part say?" I said, laughing.

"This part also turns into a recipe," said Jane, laughing with me.

About ten minutes passed. An event organizer announced that the projection would start, then read a brief introduction, using terms like "hypercontemporary" and "decontextualized online imagery" to describe the work being showcased. Everyone in the room applauded. "Hypercontemporary decontextualized online imagery" was what this crowd wanted.

A GIF appeared on screen featuring a crude-looking, macho warrior rendered in 3D running in front of a psychedelic background. Most people in the room laughed or chuckled. Though the visual style was somewhat reminiscent of early 3D video games, the GIF looked more like the product of a rendering test gone wrong, a sort of happy accident. Post-internet art often employed a nostalgia-as-novelty approach, the result of a generation whose definition of art included Newgrounds.com, Microsoft Word clip art and *Goldeneye 007* for Nintendo 64.

As the projection went on, I began to feel like the GIFs weren't having any effect on me. It was like I was oversaturated, as if my brain was suffering from a kind of eating disorder that prevented it from being able to ingest art. "I've seen too much," I thought, mentally picturing a grizzled war veteran returning home from the front lines, unable to readjust to civilian life.

13

Staring at my own Tumblr account, I absent-mindedly looked for the "Unfollow" button.

14

It was always "the hottest year on record."

15

What is art except being the real estate agent of your own neuroses.

16

The best way to survive on no money was to give up. You could teach yourself to never buy anything, own only one pair of pants, use duct tape to fix whatever's broken, download all your entertainment from the internet for free, give yourself haircuts, rent forever, date forever, put ketchup on everything, function without a driver's license, walk in the rain instead of purchasing an umbrella.

While making rice in my kitchen, I thought about Grace's relationship to food compared to mine. Grace liked purchasing organic products, studying menus of restaurants online, watching documentaries about evil food corporations trying to enslave humanity. One of her favourite television shows was *MasterChef*, a culinary competition in which the main objective was to avoid getting yelled at by celebrity chef Gordon Ramsay. Compared to her, my relationship to food was mathematical. Eating for me was mostly an annoyance, something I wanted to get rid of so that I could spend more time working. Early into our relationship, Grace had asked me what my "favourite food" was and I had replied, "I don't know," because at that moment, I honestly couldn't remember the last time I had eaten for pleasure.

My cat, a one-year-old female named Battle, began asking for food, so I walked to the fridge and opened a can of cat food that I had shoplifted from a large retail store. To save money, I sometimes avoided paying for things like multivitamins or fruits at the supermarket. It felt like a kind of philanthropy, as if the Provigo closest to my apartment was supporting the arts by allowing me to steal cat food from it.

"Thank you for your patronage," I wanted to tell the security guard on my way out.

I lived alone in a small apartment on Clark, near Duluth, didn't own much, liked it that way. Before the internet era, you had to look at reality more. Now, reality could appear underwhelming and you would barely notice, as what you truly paid attention to wasn't reality, but what appeared on your computer screen.

Overall, I was someone who was "happy with little," yet somehow never fully satisfied with any of my career accomplishments.

Eating food at my desk a few minutes later, I watched a YouTube video from the Game Grumps' channel, then replied to an email from a potential client. "How long can I really keep up this freelancing thing?" I thought. "I'll be fine just as long as my health never fails and I am a robot," I thought. I refreshed my email account and saw that I had just received a payment for a freelancing contract I had completed about ten months before. "$300," I thought. I briefly felt wealthy and prosperous, like I was part of the 1%. I felt like I was Snoop Dogg. "Is Snoop Dogg part of the 1%?" I thought.

Eventually, the feeling of wealth evaporated into the afternoon and then I was myself again.

Later that day, I changed my desktop background from a rendering of the Milky Way to a picture of Mount Fuji. "The Milky Way and Mount Fuji exist for the sole purpose of me having a beautiful desktop background," I thought. Checking Facebook, I saw a message from Eloise, which contained a link to a job ad that a friend of hers had posted. The position was in Toronto, involved website management, photo editing, social media and graphic design. "In case you're interested," Eloise had added.

"That would be perfect," I typed. Without overthinking, I dusted off my résumé from a folder on my hard drive, filled out an online job application and pressed the send button. A few minutes later, I found myself scanning job websites like Indeed.ca and Workopolis, looking for similar Toronto-based positions I could apply for. All of a sudden, I began to feel like moving to Ontario was no longer an imaginary project, but a concrete plan that I was setting in motion, or maybe had set in motion a long time ago without realizing.

"I have to do it," I thought. "I have to dynamite my life and move to Toronto. I'll get new opportunities there. I'll feel inspired again."

With a sense of remoteness, I began thinking about Grace, then about the overall trajectory of my life up to this point. I visualized myself at a junction between two separate future timelines. In the first timeline, I decided that I had no interest in starting a family, which would take time, resources and energy away from art. In this timeline, it seemed cruel to stay in a relationship with Grace if our long-term goals were incompatible. I would break up with her, use Toronto as a kind of fugue state, then remain without major financial commitments for the rest of my life, alone and moderately productive. Meanwhile, Grace would probably stay in Montreal, study physical therapy, graduate, then maybe move back to Newfoundland, hoping to finally meet someone stable she could settle down with, someone less self-involved.

In the second timeline, I decided that it would be foolish of me to let go of Grace, as she was, in fact, the romantic partner I had always wanted, but had simply given up looking for. In this timeline, I somehow managed to convince Grace to relocate to Toronto to study physical therapy, then continued pursuing art as best as I could while receiving love and support from her. Over time, our lives would become slowly intertwined, like two rivers flowing into one another. Several years would pass. Maybe we would move back to Montreal. In our late thirties, we would make one human baby together as a compromise between her ideals and mine, maybe acquire property, feel what normal people feel.

"What if the second timeline is the one that's real life?" I thought.

Still, I couldn't help feeling like there was something powerful about choosing the first timeline, about rejecting acceptance. I imagined organizing a formal ceremony, inviting all my friends, making an official announcement. "Thank you for coming, everyone," I would say, raising a glass of wine. "I'd like to make an announcement: I never want to have babies. It's okay if I end up becoming a weird loner. Let's all celebrate."

17

Consciousness was a nightmare.

18

An anagram for "delusional artist" was "rationalised lust."

19

If god was real, he would technically be an overworked, under-paid freelancer.

20

"I found it in one of the cupboards," I overheard Andrea say. She was talking to Grace and wearing, for some reason, a coffee filter as a hat. I wasn't paying attention to their conversation too much, felt instead oddly mesmerized by Grace, watching her face update itself in real-time with various expressions, her facial muscles re-engineering her skin, her eyebrows folding and then unfolding, like pliable chairs.

It was eight hours later and I was at a loft party in Griffin-town, on the second floor of a normal-looking, though appar-ently noise-friendly apartment building. In a corner of the main room, an unattended laptop was connected to a pair of speakers and functioned as a self-service DJ station. The loft was decorated with unusual items, like a glass lamp in the shape of a tulip or a sheet of bubble wrap duct-taped to a wall. I had joined this party late and was there not to socialize, but to see Grace. I was planning to tell her that I had officially decided to move to Toronto, only she was already two or three drinks ahead of me, seemed to be in a good place and grateful to be spending time with her friends.

I didn't want to spoil her night, and so decided to wait.

"Do you want to taste?" said Grace about a minute later, drawing attention to the small aluminum can in her right hand.

I asked her what the drink was and she replied, "Margarita beer." The can's packaging seemed overly festive, as if it was partying without me.

"I don't really like it," Grace added. "It's too sweet. But it was on sale and I am kind of drunk now, so I guess mission accomplished."

"How was today?" I said.

"Fine," said Grace. She paused. "It was just, it was normal."

She paused again. I sensed that she wanted to entertain me by talking about her day in an interesting manner, but was working with sub-par material, like a movie director trying to salvage a bad script. Ashlyn, who was sporting a striped t-shirt and a neon pink baseball cap, joined our conversation. She told Grace she had messaged her a few hours before about going for Indian food, but hadn't heard back.

"Did you finally get the camera on your phone fixed, by the way?" said Ashlyn.

"Hopefully soon," said Grace. "I just don't have the money right now, but I am supposed to get more shifts in July."

"You should trade your cat for a new iPhone," I said.

"I don't know if they would go for that," said Grace. "Maybe if it was your cat. You guys should see Daniel's cat, Battle. She's so cute and little."

"Oh, come on," said Ashlyn. "Tom-Tom is super funny. The Apple people would love him."

"Tom-Tom would sell more iPhones than Steve Jobs," I said.

"I don't know about that," said Grace. "My cat doesn't do anything. He just stares out the window for hours even when nothing's happening out there. He's really into it. It's like he's watching a big action movie."

"*Transformers*," I said.

"Yeah," said Grace. "It's like he's watching *Transformers*."

Two sentences later, Grace said the word, "iPhone" again and my phone vibrated at the same time. I glanced at the screen and said, "Jane's coming," aloud without realizing that I was talking.

"Do you know if Elliot is with her?" said Ashlyn. "I love Elliot. He looks like a wizard. A young wizard. Like he could be in Harry Potter."

"You and Jane are so funny together," said Andrea. "I don't mean this negatively, I just don't understand your friendship. In a good way."

"In a good way," I thought, and then wondered if simply adding the words "in a good way" at the end of any sentence could allow you to say more or less anything to anyone. "All your priorities in life seem completely insane to me," I pictured myself saying to an imaginary person. "In a good way."

"No, it's true," I said. "My friendship with Jane doesn't make sense at all. In a good way."

"She's such a free spirit," said Ashlyn. "She has all this positive energy and is into nature and planets and magic. You're, like, more logical. It's like if a bong and a computer were best friends."

Ashlyn's joke made everyone laugh, including me.

"When I first met Jane, I thought her close friends would be, like, hot art babes," said Grace. "Not that you're not a hot art babe in your own way, but you know what I mean."

Andrea shifted to her right to make room for Roberto and Derek. I briefly stared at Derek's t-shirt, which was green and featured the logo of the company Lacoste. "I hope it's a size small," I thought, abstractly imagining myself inheriting the shirt from him in the future. I began chatting with Roberto about a YouTube video we had both seen that featured a German shepherd shovelling a driveway in the winter. "Yo, it's crazy," Roberto said, laughing and smiling. In the last few months, he had begun integrating expressions like "Yo" and "I'm down" into his English vocabulary. "In my mind, this is how I imagine Newfoundland," he added. "Big dogs shovelling the driveways."

Changing the conversation topic, Roberto asked about my art videos, mentioning that he wasn't sure what the term "post-internet" meant. I tried to explain that it was pretty much an all-purpose term used to describe art aware that it exists "after" the internet, but Roberto didn't seem to follow. Instead, he waited for me to finish talking and then looked at me and said, "Wow," in a neutral tone. Though Roberto's English was generally decent, he sometimes seemed to lose track of conversations. His trick, when that happened, was to reply something generic like "wow" or "no way," pretending to be impressed by what the other person had just said, regardless of what it was.

As a result, Roberto often said "wow" or "no way" as a response to banal or unremarkable statements.

About fifteen minutes passed. Still chatting with Roberto, I was surprise-hugged from behind by Jane, which caused me to flinch and try to evade the hug, almost hitting her by accident.

"Thank god you didn't head-butt me," said Jane, laughing. She was wearing a floral print dress and silver half-moon earrings, with a small jewel sticker on her right temple.

"Sorry if I moved," I said, also laughing.

"It's okay," said Jane. "It's just funny. Can you imagine if you had sent me into a prolonged coma?"

"You wouldn't have been able to attend your art night next week," I said.

"What's that movie where the guy is in a coma and he can only communicate by blinking?" said Jane. "I could have talked to people that way. Through eye twitches."

"You're thinking of *The Diving Bell and the Butterfly*, I believe," said Elliot, who was standing behind her. "Although he's not in a coma. It was just a stroke."

"Is that what it was?" said Jane. "Anyway. How's everyone doing?"

"Good," said Grace. "I am pretty drunk."

"Everyone here looks wasted," said Jane, grinning. "I don't know what's going on. Elliot has MDMA for sale if you guys want."

"I could be into it," said Grace. "I am working tomorrow, though. Wait, let me think about it."

"I still owe you $10 from two weeks ago," said Jane to me. "Do you want me to give you MDMA instead? I can give you cash as well, either one is fine with me. It's up to you."

"I kind of need the money," I said, "so I should probably take that. But it feels like the MDMA is worth more."

"Take the drug," said Jane. "Get wasted!"

"I'll do drugs if you do some," said Grace. "I don't have to be at work until mid-afternoon tomorrow, so it should be okay."

"I think we've decided that we're doing this," I said.

"Great," said Jane. About a minute later, Elliot placed a small amount of powder in the palm of my hand, then in Grace's. I licked my hand, then drowned the hostile taste in margarita beer.

"We haven't tried it yet, but it's supposed to be good," said Jane before asking Ashlyn if she wanted to go smoke on the balcony. Grace left to go look for a bathroom.

"You should have this," said Andrea, placing the coffee filter on my head. "You're officially on drugs now. This is the perfect hat for someone who's on drugs. Trust me, I know fashion."

"I trust you," I said. "I don't know how we got to that point. I didn't even want to come to this thing."

"This party is strange," said Andrea. "Or maybe I am just not that into it tonight. I usually don't mind being single, but it's been harder lately. It feels like all my friends are in great relationships all of a sudden. Ashlyn and Roberto. You and Grace."

"Val isn't," I said.

"Well, yeah, that's true," said Andrea, pausing. "Do you ever wonder how people you see at parties all the time are going to age?"

"What do you mean?" I said.

"Like if everyone is going to age horribly?" said Andrea.

"I don't know," I said. "I hope someone tells me when I've aged horribly."

"I'll tell you," said Andrea. "I'll be nice about it."

"I am counting on you," I said. "Maybe we should have a reunion ten years from now. Like a high school reunion, only it's a sketchy party reunion."

"That sounds good," said Andrea. "Actually, no, wait, that sounds brutal."

I continued chatting with Andrea while quickly finishing a beer, then starting another. Loud rap music gradually replaced regular rap music. Later, I stumbled into a conversation with Cal, who was wearing a gray tank top. I didn't know anything about him, except for the fact that he was in a band with Elliot and liked wearing gray tank tops.

"So wait, what do you do in Montreal?" I said. "Are you still in school? I don't think I know this."

"Oh, no, I am done school," said Cal. "I am just working right now."

"As a lawyer," I said.

"What?" said Cal. "I am not a lawyer. Why would I be a lawyer?"

"I don't know why I said that," I said. "I was just kidding."

"No, wait, I take it back," said Cal. "I am definitely a lawyer. I can pull it off."

"I need legal advice," I said.

"Sue them," said Cal.

"Do you think I should?" I said.

"Yes," said Cal. "Absolutely. This is my legal opinion: Sue everyone. Sue society. For malpractice."

"Alright, I am suing," I said. "You're good at this."

"Top of my class at lawyer night school," said Cal. "Wait, where's my beer?"

Checking my phone, I saw that about an hour had passed. I was starting to feel drunk, but also headachey and disoriented. My body had fully absorbed the MDMA, though what I was experiencing wasn't manic euphoria, but a kind of jitteriness mixed with discomfort, an unfocused anger directed at nothing in particular. Exploring the loft suddenly seemed choppy and more difficult, as if reality was now a high-definition video game running on outdated hardware. "Why did I do drugs?" I thought. "This is so mediocre."

Wanting to escape the party, I walked to the other side of the room and opened a door, which I thought would lead me to the hallway. To my amazement, what I found behind the door wasn't the hallway, but a closet that contained several jackets, an umbrella, a broom and a shoebox. "Where did the hallway go?" I thought, standing paralyzed in front of the jackets, one of which was extremely yellow. "How did the hallway get replaced with a closet? Can I still exit this party? What if I am trapped in here forever?"

This ridiculous situation, in which the loft's only exit had somehow been magically replaced with a closet, began to resemble a kind of escalating mental crisis, one that seemed both amusing and life threatening.

Trying and failing to come up with a new plan to exit the room, I began to feel as if my anxiety was having an orgasm.

"What are you doing?" said Jane, appearing to my left.

"I can't find the exit," I said, sounding weak and defenseless, like a baby animal born naked and blind.

"What do you mean?" said Jane. "It's right there."

She pointed in the direction of another door, which, upon closer inspection, was obviously the one I had been looking for. "Oh," I said aloud. "Never mind."

Outside the building, I found Grace sitting on the sidewalk and chatting with Ashlyn. She asked me how I was feeling and I replied, "Shitty."

"I feel shitty too," said Grace. "I don't know what Elliot gave us, but that wasn't MDMA. It might have been bath salts mixed with something else."

"I don't want to go back in," I said. "I am, like, afraid now."

"We can leave," said Grace.

"Are you sure?" I said. "I would go, but you can stay if you want."

"No, let's go," said Grace.

Several minutes later, we said goodbye to Ashlyn and began walking towards Grace's apartment. We crossed a street and I had to stop to throw up what looked like a black substance.

"That was dumb," I said, spitting on the ground.

"What was?" said Grace.

"Partying," I said. "Partying is dumb. I feel like I want to go on a party hiatus for a while. I don't want to drink and I don't want to party."

"We can do that," said Grace. "We can do a party hiatus. There are other things we can do than partying."

"Like what?" I said.

"Like," said Grace. "I don't know. Something."

Grace mentioned wanting to hail a cab, but we walked for a long time in the general direction of her apartment without encountering one. Eventually, about an hour and a half later, we made it all the way to her doorstep, entered her apartment and both collapsed on her bed. It was a little after 4 a.m. and Grace looked exhausted, though still obeyed her bedtime ritual of smoking weed before going to sleep. I watched her roll a joint for about a minute and then fell into a dreamless hole.

21

I woke up lying on my side with my entire body, including my head, buried under a blanket. In my sleep, I would often pull a blanket over me without noticing. Grace had made fun of me for this in the past, a quirk I had developed during my childhood, but I liked how we both had sleeping rituals. She needed to sedate herself with weed to fall asleep, while I liked to hide and disappear.

"An artist who likes to hide and disappear," I thought.

From a distance, I could hear sirens wailing, with the noise becoming sharper and exponentially louder over time. I felt like I was being yelled at in a foreign language. I looked up and stared vacantly at Tom-Tom for a few seconds, vaguely hoping that the cat would calmly provide an explanation of what was going on.

"What are these sirens?" half-said, half-mumbled Grace. "They're nonstop. This is so unpleasant."

"I have no idea," I said, reaching for the plastic bottle on her nightstand. I drank water from it and then passed it to Grace.

"What are they doing out there?" she said.

"I don't know, fire trucks putting out a fire maybe," I said. "Some sort of loud fire."

"Ugh," said Grace. "We need more water. I am still thirsty, but I don't want to get up. I kind of wish the fire trucks would come in here."

"That would be good," I said. "Burst through the front window, spray us a little."

"I'll go refill the bottle," said Grace.

"No, I'll get up," I said. "I got this."

"Are you sure?" said Grace. "It's fine."

"No, I want to," I said.

"Well, if you want to," said Grace, smiling. I grabbed the water bottle, got up and walked to the kitchen. Moving my body around felt perilous, like driving a car through a storm. Replenishing our water supply, I replayed events from the night before in my head and then remembered still having to discuss moving to Toronto with Grace. "Shit," I thought. "Do we really have to talk about this now? I just feel like staring at a wall for the next six hours," I thought. "Where's the closest wall?" I thought.

Back in Grace's room, I saw that she was now composing a text message, her thumbs moving in precise little motions with good concentration and speed, like some sort of compact martial art. I placed the plastic bottle on the nightstand and sat next to her on the bed.

"So we should talk about something," I said. "I wanted to tell you last night, but then you looked like you were having fun, so I decided to hold off."

"Okay," said Grace. "Well, what is it?"

"We've talked about this before," I said, unintentionally pausing dramatically a little. "I decided that I am officially moving to Toronto. I just feel like it'll be good for me to be in a new environment. I am going to try to move there for August."

There was a second pause. I looked directly at Grace, couldn't help noticing the way her face was updating itself, her expression changing from smiling and distracted to focused and engaged.

"I am not surprised," she said. "I mean, I knew it could happen. You hadn't brought it up in a while, though, so I was kind of hoping that maybe you didn't want to go anymore."

"I wasn't sure," I said. "I didn't want to tell you, 'I am leaving' and then change my mind and go, 'No, just kidding, I am staying.' I didn't think that was fair to you."

"No, and thank you, but I am still disappointed that you want to go," said Grace.

"I understand," I said. "We should talk about what that means for us, I guess."

"Toronto is only five hours away, and if I can't get into physical therapy at McGill, I might have to move there next year to study anyway," said Grace. "We could continue to date long distance, if you're okay with that."

"Are you sure this is what you want?" I said. "Long distance, I mean. It's a lot of the disadvantages without most of the advantages."

"Wait, what do you think this means for us?" said Grace.

"I am not sure," I said, "but my fear is that as soon as I am no longer in Montreal, it'll be like I am on another planet."

"I would be willing to make this work, but you have to be on board," said Grace.

"I know this isn't what you want, but I think we should break up at the end of the month and try to stay on good terms," I said. "We wouldn't be boyfriend and girlfriend anymore, but I would still help you and support you if I can. It's not like something bad has happened and I don't want to talk to you anymore. I have no reason to stop caring about you."

"That makes it way worse," said Grace, raising her voice.

"Probably," I said. "I am sorry if this is bad news. I've been bored with Montreal lately, so I feel like if I were to stay here, I would continue to do the same things over and over again and grow frustrated and then project that frustration onto you. If I don't want to be in Montreal anymore, then I'd rather not stay. I'd rather move to Toronto and see what happens to my life there."

"I don't want you to be unhappy," said Grace, "and I think I understand why you want to go, so it's not that."

"Even if we're not dating anymore, we can still get along," I said. "We naturally get along. That's why we rarely fight."

"It's been really great for me," said Grace. "I mean, I let you see me with no makeup on, which is rare for me, even at the boyfriend level. I still don't let my dad see me without anything on, because he used to make me feel so bad about my skin. Last night, I was just rambling on to Ashlyn about how good to me you've been. She told me that she thought you were the perfect boyfriend for me. I said, 'I wouldn't say perfect, but close enough.'"

"Do you think your friends will understand?" I said. "Why I am leaving, I mean. I don't want to be, like, the villain or something."

"I am sure they will," said Grace. "They'll probably take my side, but I don't think they'll be mad at you or anything."

"Good," I said. "I worry about that."

"So what you're saying is that you're leaving in four weeks?" said Grace.

"Yeah," I said. "We should probably talk about this again when you've had time to process things."

"Again, I am sorry if this is bad news."

Grace didn't respond. I said, "I'll just go for now," and gathered my things and left. Exiting her apartment building, I was greeted by a crushing amount of sunlight and loud sirens blaring from afar. I walked in the direction of my apartment with my eyes unable to recalibrate themselves, vaguely yearning for a button that would allow me to lower reality's brightness, like what you would find on a laptop. On Mont-Royal, I saw that a convoy of fire trucks was slowly parading through the streets. Tiny children accompanying the firemen were wearing red helmets and waving at people on the ground.

My hangover failed to find the parade amusing or cute.

22

"Blame men," read Eloise's Facebook status.

23

Wondering if my internet presence was only giving me the illusion of career progress, instead of actual progress.

24

Walking into an art gallery, I thought about going on a "party hiatus" again. It seemed like the kind of good idea that would also be practical, as it meant I would be wasting less money overall. The only downside was that I wasn't sure what would replace partying in my life.

DHC/ART, the art gallery, was presenting work by a Brooklyn-based artist named Cory Arcangel, who played "serious pranks with computers," according to a description on DHC's website. I was already familiar with some of his work, including *Permanent Vacation*, from 2008, in which two computers trapped in an infinite loop sent one another automatic out-of-office replies back and forth, and *Self Playing Nintendo 64 NBA Courtside 2*, from 2011, in which a "self-playing" Nintendo 64 console displayed a low-polygon Shaquille O'Neal attempting free throws and missing the basket over and over again. Though a lot of the material on display was also available online, there was something satisfying about seeing these pieces in person, simple sensory pleasures such as the way the physical space allowed for sound effects from one piece, like Shaquille O'Neal flatly dribbling a basketball, to combine with sound from another. Presenting my videos online often made me feel as if they existed outside of time and space. Anyone could watch them at any time, but then why would they? They could watch them at any time, including later. From that perspective, exhibiting my work in a physical space felt like tethering it to reality, giving it a reason to exist by attaching it to a precise time and place.

"Art is ridiculous," I thought, leaving the gallery an hour later. "Art is ridiculous and I have to be the best at it."

25

The Craigslist page for apartment listings in Toronto felt hectic and fast moving, like some sort of international stock market. Toronto,

I knew, was experiencing a "rent crisis," meaning apartments were more expensive to rent than in Montreal and generally impossible to find. I was replying to ads, sending waves and waves of emails, but wasn't receiving many responses. Eventually, I exchanged a series of diplomatic emails with someone named Devin and was able to convince him to interview me over Skype for a room available in a three-bedroom apartment. This seemed like a good idea until we ran into technical problems. Devin's microphone wasn't working properly, which meant he was able to hear me, but I couldn't hear him. Because of this, our conversation was stilted and awkward, as Devin couldn't answer me directly, had to pause and respond by manually typing sentences into a chat box. I had to do most of the talking, and the one-way conversation with Devin felt a little like being a television news anchor reading news items unidirectionally to a camera.

"It feels lonely," I thought. "Television news anchors must feel lonely."

Later, I was told the room would be given to another applicant.

26

Buying fish at the grocery store, I thought about how my lifestyle was only possible because of my participation in a gigantic, worldwide system of exploitation and bullying that kept the price of various items at the supermarket relatively affordable for consumers in North America. Me purchasing tilapia at a convenient price point meant someone, somewhere else, was inevitably getting short-changed, though did I owe anything to that person? Or was the best thing I could do for that person what I was already doing, which was to live my life like a bed bug of capitalism?

27

I wanted to contact Grace, who I hadn't talked to since our conversation about me moving, but wasn't sure if I should give her more time. About two hours later, I received a text message from her complaining about Dom, her twenty-four-year-old manager at work, who, I knew, routinely abused his power, seemed to enjoy making a public display of it, as if yelling at his employees was a special attraction for visitors, like the birth of a panda bear in captivity.

"He's such a little bitch sometimes," said Grace about thirty minutes later. We were sitting on her bed and she was rummaging through her purse, looking for rolling papers. Through the walls, I could hear Grace's roommate listening to what seemed to be a podcast about jogging and fitness. "I am usually on his good side, so I don't get screamed at too much, but today was awful."

"What did he yell at you for?" I said.

"For sneezing," said Grace. "I was having allergies for whatever reason, so I sneezed twice in a row, but I was nowhere near food. He got upset and lectured me in front of everyone, telling me I was being 'unprofessional' and all of that."

"He yelled at you for sneezing?" I said.

"Yeah," said Grace. "It wasn't a quiet sneeze, but it didn't seem like anyone cared. You've heard me sneeze before. I sound kind of like a dog when I am sneezing."

"I know," I said. "I love dogs."

I wanted to make Grace smile, but she frowned instead.

"Wait," I said. "That came out wrong. I wasn't calling you a dog, I just meant that you sound cute when you're sneezing."

"Thanks," said Grace sarcastically. "Anyway. Sorry if I am just venting about Dom. It's so stupid."

"It's okay," I said. "I don't mind."

We continued chatting in a relaxed manner. Grace smoked weed, seemed to feel better. "I've been sleeping way too much lately," I said. "I feel like I am in the 1% of sleeping, like my sleep hours should trickle down onto other people." Later, we watched a *Vice* documentary about climate change titled *The World is Sinking*, which was both alarming and depressing. After the program ended, Grace rested her head on my chest and thanked me for coming and I said, "Of course," and we hugged.

Then we kissed.

Then we had sex and said, "I love you," to one another afterwards and meant it.

28

Behind Roberto, I could see two people smiling while looking at my videos. It was a week later and we were attending Jane's art night, with Roberto drinking a beer and me drinking vitamin water, as I had officially decided to do the party hiatus. Being sober around people felt like a kind of injury, as if I should be wearing a dog cone to prevent me from hurting myself while talking to someone. I quickly became hyper-conscious of how much I had been using alcohol as a way of making myself less anxious around people. Since I only drank in social settings, and almost never alone, I didn't see myself as an alcoholic, didn't think I had any dependency on alcohol.

The videos I was presenting that night had all been created

using 3D video games that I had modified or manipulated to generate glitches and other irregular behaviours. Technology, I thought, was always at its most fascinating when it was about to reach its breaking point, and a glitch could be used to express how odd regular, everyday life sometimes felt. Deliberately pushing technology to its limits was a kind of sadism maybe, though it never failed to create interesting accidents, as most video games were often only a glitch away from looking nightmarish.

To put together my videos, I would record footage of my-self playing the modified games, sometimes staging intri-cate scenarios, and then assemble the different clips into a short film, usually adding things like text captions, a new sound-track or home-recorded voiceovers. I was trying to push the narrative component of my videos a little further, had started including intimate or personal elements to give them more emotional resonance. In the end, my videos were strange, un-predictable, occasionally funny, and typically produced a positive reaction. Like all artists, I sometimes saw myself as a genius, and some-times as a fraud.

Exploring the gallery with Roberto, I glanced at works by other artists, which felt a little like scrolling through Tumblr. There was a little bit of everything on display, a salad bar of videos, illustrations and even a few paintings on a wall. I liked some pieces, though most seemed average to me. One painting was titled *Memory* and featured, according to a small card located below the canvas, "the language of online communities" and "the influence of digital means of production." "That title seems really lazy," I thought. "You could give any painting a generic title like *Memory*."

Wondering if my theory was true, I began looking around the room, pretending that every art object around me was titled *Memory*.

"*Memory*," I thought, staring at a black-and-white video of attractive women swimming in a pool in slow motion.

Though there was free wine left and I felt tempted to drink, I was able to persuade myself to walk away from the makeshift bar. I asked Roberto what he thought of the works on display and he replied that he liked "everything." As a person, Roberto was overwhelmingly nice and well intentioned, the complete opposite, maybe, of screaming celebrity chef Gordon Ramsay. He was someone who had, somehow, never learned malice, the same way some people never learn how to swim. Ashlyn sometimes complained that he was "allergic" to conflict, would always try to diffuse arguments by laughing things off, which made her even angrier when she was upset with him.

Because he didn't have much of a web presence and rarely bragged about his work, Roberto was easy to underestimate. He was, in fact, a very talented 3D modeller and animator, skills he had taught himself by watching tutorials online. I liked his perspective, enjoyed asking him what he thought of different artworks, though I usually had to encourage him to make negative comments.

Since his visa didn't allow him to work legally in Canada, Roberto made money by taking freelance projects, plus washing dishes three days per week at a restaurant that paid him under the table. The Mexican family who owned the restaurant treated him well, but the work itself was demanding, and Roberto didn't feel like he was particularly well suited for it. Chatting with him was usually a good reminder that even though I viewed myself as "poor," there were much lower levels of poverty I had never experienced. Compared to other people's situations, my poverty was a luxury cruise ship. Even worse, my poverty was self-appointed. As a reasonably educated white man living in Canada, I could probably make a little more money simply by compromising more and playing by the rules.

"Self-appointed poverty," I thought. "Who would choose that?"

About an hour passed. Jane instructed everyone to gather on one side of the room for her live performance. She connected her laptop to a projector, replacing the black-and-white women in slow motion, then informed the crowd that her presentation was going to be "very minimal." "I wanted to do something way more elaborate, but I ran out of time," she said.

"This is called *The dead are dead,*" Jane added.

On her computer, she opened a web browser and typed the address "findagrave.com." The website, she explained, docu-mented famous and less famous graves from around the world and functioned "kind of like a Facebook for dead people." She used the search engine to locate various graves and then read curious, but seemingly sincere comments left by anonymous internet users. "We miss you," read a user comment written below the digital grave of a Japanese novelist who had passed away in 1927. After reading several messages left below various graves, all of which were sweet and earnest and made the audience laugh, Jane asked the crowd what they thought of the user comments, which triggered a group discussion on mourning in relation to social media.

After Jane's presentation, everyone got up and resumed chatting. I asked Jane if she was happy with her performance and she replied that "it was what it was."

"It was simple, but I thought it was good," I said.

"I wasn't going for anything flashy," said Jane. "I wanted to do the moon thing, but I chickened out. I don't know why I chickened out. Are you sticking around for a bit? You should. Pretty soon you'll be in Toronto, so I won't get to see you any-more."

"I am meeting Grace at her apartment later, but she's at work now, so I can stay for a while," I said.

"Good," said Jane. "What's happening with you and Grace, by the way? What's going on there?"

"I am not even sure," I said. "We discussed breaking up and didn't talk for a few days. Then we hung out and had sex and now we're spending pretty much all of our free time together. I am impressed by how she's handling things. She's supportive and helping me prepare to move and stuff."

"Well, I am sure you know this," said Jane, "but be careful or you might end up hurting Grace."

29

"It's so hot tonight," said Grace, who was watching ASMR videos on her laptop. It was three hours later and I had just arrived at her apartment. The electric fan next to her bed was oscillating loudly, as if trying to emasculate the fan inside her laptop.

"I know," I said. "Look at how much I am sweating. I am like a rainforest right now."

"Take off your shirt and pants," said Grace.

"Oh right, I don't have to wear pants anymore," I said.

Before undressing, I handed Grace a small paper bag. "Here, this is for you," I said. Inside the bag was a yellow cupcake decorated with white sprinkles.

"You brought me a cupcake?" said Grace. "Aw, that's sweet of you."

"They had a few left when I was leaving," I said. "I couldn't drink free wine, so I had to get free something."

"That's only fair," said Grace.

"Socializing without drinking was insane," I said. "You know how when you break your right hand and then you have to relearn how to do everything with the other hand? It felt like that."

"Maybe it'll get better," said Grace, taking a bite from the cupcake. I noticed she was wearing a light blue bracelet, so I asked where it was from and she said a co-worker had given it to her, as he had attended a Moroccan wedding the weekend before.

"Is that really a thing?" I said. "They give away bracelets at Moroccan weddings?"

"I guess," said Grace.

"I was going to stay, 'That's strange,' but it's probably just as weird as hurling rice at people," I said.

"Right," said Grace. "Before I forget, you still haven't found anyone to take over your apartment, right? Val was telling me that she's tired of living with people. She might be interested in taking over, if you're moving."

"She should definitely come visit," I said. "That would be great."

"I thought so," said Grace before finishing the cupcake.

I sat on the bed next to her and we kissed. I placed my arm around her, pulled her towards me and said, "Come here."

"I am here," said Grace. "I am right next to you."

"No, I mean, 'here,'" I said, laughing and pulling her even closer, our faces touching. I became conscious that what I meant by the word "here" was inside my skull, which is where I really was. Grace climbed on top of me, with her hair coming down to cover her face. I wanted to put her hair aside with my hand to see her more clearly, but she prevented me from doing so.

"I am trying to cover my forehead with my bangs," said Grace.

"I guess I am not being very subtle. I've been stressed lately, so I had breakouts. I am not sure I want you to look at my forehead."

"Show me," I said. "We've been over this. I honestly don't care."

"I know you don't," said Grace.

"Wait, are you stressed because of me?" I said.

"Well, yeah," said Grace. "You're leaving."

"I am," I said, "but I don't know."

"What do you mean?" said Grace.

"I've been thinking about the break-up thing," I said. "I thought we were going to fight about me moving, but now it seems like it's the opposite that's happening. I just felt really good being around you this week."

Grace smiled.

"I felt good too," she said.

"Don't tell anyone, but I think I am, like, happy," I said. "I am not happy in Montreal right now, but I am happy in this."

"Well," said Grace, "we could at least try dating long distance, and if it really doesn't work, then we would know."

"I feel like we should do that," I said. "Would you be okay with that?"

"Obviously," said Grace, sounding emotional.

"Long distance," I said.

"You'll be great at long distance," said Grace. "You already live inside your computer. I don't know why you're worried this won't work out."

"I am sorry if you were stressed," I said.

"It's okay," said Grace. "I am fine now. I kept thinking, 'Maybe he thinks I am boring. Maybe we've dated long enough and he thinks we don't have a future together. Maybe he thinks I talk too much.'"

"I don't think you're boring," I said. "Don't shit-talk yourself."

"I went over to Ashlyn's today and we had coffee," said Grace. "She kept saying, 'If this was my boyfriend, I'd be so mad at him for wanting to break up.' She wanted me to write you a letter."

"I told you that was going to happen," I said. "I am the villain."

"She was just being protective of me," said Grace, her voice quivering a little.

"Are you crying?" I said.

"No, shut up," said Grace, wiping away a tear. "There's just, there's a feeling in my eye."

"A feeling in your eye," I said, laughing a little.

"That's not what meant," said Grace. "Anyway. I am happy."

CHAPTER TWO

Tell My Dreams
to Give Me Up

"Is it just me or are most artists today incredibly retarded?" read the first paragraph of an article on *Vice* Canada in which I was both mentioned by name and referred to as "some guy." "Look, I can appreciate a fine painting, but what I can't appreciate is that a lot of artists emerging from the easily distracted generation don't even seem to do anything anymore. I am calling it now: this internet art, new media whatever bullshit has got to stop. It's 2013 and nobody is asking for this. It's not 'contemporary,' it's lazy and dumb and pointless and boring. For instance, I recently spent a week in one of our nation's most romanticized destinations, Montreal, and was dragged to an 'art night' featuring the work of talented local artists like Gavin Fisher, Jane Hatherley and Daniel Kerry (By 'talented,' of course, I mean 'clueless' and 'dopey-looking.') I don't mean to pick on the little guy here, but I really feel like someone needs to drop some real talk on these assholes: Guys, all of it sucked. First of all, your show was called *Eternity Now*, which is a horrible title and you should never title anything that. Second, your bad drawings and bad paintings were surrounded by bad prints of computer screenshots or whatever and accompanied by bad videos of some guy farting around in *Fallout 3* or something. What is this? Am I supposed to look at this shit and have a goddamn profound experience of art? How entitled can you be to think that this crap deserves our time and attention? Sorry it was such a fucking chore for you guys to make art, but why are you all taking it out on me?"

"Which cat is it?" asked a disoriented Grace. Next to her, Tom-

Tom was purring aggressively, applying pressure on the blanket with his paws.

"It's the big cat," I said.

"Hi big cat," said Grace, petting Tom-Tom a little.

"It doesn't sound like he's purring," I said. "It sounds like he's polishing rocks inside his body or something."

"Yeah, he purrs really hard," said Grace. "He's such a gentleman, though. He's so nice to your cat. It was a good idea to bring her here."

"I am shocked my cat is the dominant one," I said. "Your cat is, like, four times her size. I thought she would have anxiety and just hide under furniture a lot. So far, she's kind of bossing him around."

"They're starting to play a little," said Grace. "They were definitely chasing one another yesterday. They're funny together."

"We should get them cat-married," I said.

"We should," said Grace. "A Moroccan wedding."

"A Moroccan cat wedding," I said, laughing. "Free bracelets for everyone."

I petted Tom-Tom, then put my arm around Grace. It was my last week in Montreal and Grace's roommate was away on a bike trip across Europe, so we had decided to temporarily live together until the end of July, after which I would be moving to Toronto. We were referring to this as our "married couple week," though that title was starting to feel less like a joke, and more like a fact.

During the day, while Grace was at work, I usually went to cafés with my laptop. I was still going nowhere, though my lack of productivity didn't have anything to do with the negative *Vice* review. In fact, I thought the *Vice* article was kind of refreshing on the whole, in the sense that a lot of "art criticism" online was just empty praise masquerading as criticism. The *Vice* review, at least, felt like something new.

At night, Grace and I would reconvene at her apartment, where she would smoke weed, and make me watch an episode or two of *MasterChef* with her. Then we would prepare dinner together and eat a satisfying meal while sitting at her kitchen table, a ritual that seemed, to me, bizarre and alien, though not unpleasant, compared to my usual routine of eating rushed food alone while staring at my laptop.

"Is it noon?" said Grace. "It looks like noon."

"It could be," I said. "I think I'll go to my apartment this afternoon. Get more boxes."

"How many trips do you think you have left?" said Grace.

"I think this will be my last one," I said.

"Already?" said Grace. "I thought you would have more things."

"I am selling or getting rid of some stuff, so all I'll be leaving in your basement is four or five boxes," I said. "Did I tell you that Val is buying my work desk?"

"I don't think you told me, but that makes sense," said Grace. "It's kind of bittersweet that she's taking over your apartment. On one hand, she'll be living closer to me, so we'll get to hang out more often, but on the other, it'll be strange to go to your apartment and not see you there."

"I know," I said. "Things won't be the same soon. But I just have to do it. I have to blow up my life."

"It's too bad," said Grace.

03

I thought my cat was going to hate being constrained in a carrier for a long period of time, but she seemed okay with it, wasn't crying or protesting too much, was just staring at me with a nonplussed expression. It was as if she had already forgotten my apartment and Grace's apartment, had accepted the cage as her new permanent reality.

It was several days later and I was sitting in a van, with the carrier on my lap. I had booked a rideshare on Craigslist, bribing the driver an extra $10 in exchange for being allowed to have an animal with me. My plan was to bring only the strict minimum with me to Toronto, temporarily stashing the rest of my things in Grace's unfinished basement. Some of the boxes I was leaving with her contained embarrassing personal items like my high school yearbook or a gold medal I had won playing soccer as a child, but having Grace hold onto this for me felt right, like a kind of advanced trust-building exercise.

"Don't hit your sister, Ryder," said the woman sitting behind me. In the van with me were the driver, the driver's friend, a couple from France, a man sporting a bandana, the woman behind me, her teenage daughter and her energetic son, who was probably eight years old. "You apologize to her."

"No!" yelled the son, pushing the girl.

"Come on, little man," said the French woman, trying to help. "You shouldn't be so hard on your sister. Try being nice to her! You might like it."

"No!" repeated the son, hitting the girl again.

"Stop punching me," said the teenage girl, pushing the boy back.

"What are you going to do?" said the boy's mother to the French woman, sounding exasperated. "They're children."

"Yeah, but do they have to be assholes?" I thought, but refrained from saying. To distract myself, I began focusing on my memory of saying goodbye to Grace before leaving Montreal,

72

with us hugging, then her smiling and saying, "Daniel, the love of my life," before pausing and adding, "Well, so far."

Long distance, I thought, was either going to strengthen or destroy our relationship. Still, I liked Grace's approach, which seemed level-headed and pragmatic. It was as if her philosophy was, "If you love something, set it free," while my philosophy was, "If you love something, hide from it."

04

I spent my first two weeks in Toronto massively alone. I couldn't tell if I had forgotten how to meet people, or if this was a skill I had simply never acquired in the first place. Being inside my head for several days in a row felt like a kind of death, like I was progressively receding into my imagination, becoming a voice inside my own head. I was less a person, and more like the vague idea of a person, a piece of paper with an inscription on it that said, "IOU: One person."

I didn't feel lonely, or maybe I felt a tolerable amount of lonely, the way a television news anchor feels lonely.

During the day, I would walk around my new neighbourhood, feel mentally stimulated by streets I hadn't seen before, new buildings to grow bored of. In Montreal, I was so used to the layout of the streets that I would often navigate them on auto-pilot, detaching myself from my physical environment by retreating into my brain to reign over my imagination like some sort of part-time tyrant.

My new apartment was in Bracondale Hill, a quiet residential area with black squirrels and modest-looking, overpriced houses. I was subletting a room from Dana, who was in her forties, worked five or six days per week as a chef in a popular restaurant and was rarely home. She had been occupying the same apartment for many years, had a daughter roughly ten years younger than me who now lived on her own.

On the last day of my second week in Toronto, I sat on the couch in the living room and updated my LinkedIn profile for the third time in two days. Under "Honours & Awards," I briefly considered adding the gold medal I had won playing soccer as a child, as that accomplishment seemed to me just as valid as anything else I had achieved in my career so far. From a distance, I could hear Dana's pet chinchilla working out in his exercise wheel. Around me were restaurant menus, an unfinished 3,000-piece puzzle, a crate filled with old DVDs, a bookshelf, a wooden sign that said "MUST HAVE COFFEE" in angry capital letters and an unremarkable painting of a fruit platter.

"*Memory,*" I thought, giving the painting a new title in my head.

I combed through listings of what seemed like made-up jobs on job websites. One position was listed as "Social Media 2," like it was a sequel of some sort. "I just hope employers out there are desperately looking for a selfish, unmotivated, anti-social young professional with horrible worldviews," I thought.

On Tumblr, I posted a new animated GIF I had made. It wasn't much of an update, but at least it was something. My lack of productivity was making me feel like I was becoming an imaginary artist, someone who talks about making art all the time but never actually produces anything. I was afraid that if I stopped posting new content, I would lose whatever following I had gained, be quickly forgotten, as if I had never existed at all.

"How many things do I have to post on here to finally please you people?" I thought, addressing my imaginary audience in my head. Then I thought about the late '90s and making a website for the first time, how freeing and exciting the internet had felt back then. I wasn't sure when creating things had become a type of pressure.

"Are you in Toronto now?" typed Eloise on Facebook Chat. "I looked for Facebook events to invite you to, but the only thing I could find was this vernissage of yuppie artists. It's probably paintings of their condos. I didn't think you would like that."

"Thank you for trying," I typed. "How are you? You should come back, we can hang out now."

"I'll be in Toronto soon," typed Eloise, "and I am okay. I started interning at this art space called Blindside. I call it 'interning,' but it's more like volunteer work."

"That sounds good," I typed.

"It's amazing," typed Eloise. "All I have to do is help Danielle, who runs the space, organize things and handle events. I can even work there during the day. I have my own desk. Also, I don't know if this is old news by now, but I finally read that review on *Vice*."

"What did you think of it?" I typed.

"I couldn't believe how nasty it was," typed Eloise. "At the same time, it seemed so over the top and excessive. It was like someone writing a full column in the *New York Times* to publicly attack a slice of pumpkin pie. What did that pie do to you?"

"Jane was pretty upset," I typed. "I told her that the person who wrote this was deliberately trying to be as negative as possible, to make her article 'funnier.' It was a shit-on-it-first, ask-questions-later kind of approach."

"I am usually into strong female critics doing hatchet jobs, but in this case, it seems obvious that she has it all wrong," typed Eloise. "The only redeeming thing about all of this is that it's a ridiculous review from a massive publication. It's good exposure for you and Jane. You guys should embrace it."

"Yeah," I typed. "Maybe *Better Homes & Gardens* magazine will be shit-talking us next."

"Or *Men's Health*," typed Eloise. "I'd love to be featured in *Men's Health*. Talk to men about what's wrong with men."

"Did you see that guy in the comments section who called Jane dumb and said that what she was doing 'wasn't art,'" I typed, "like he had the authority to decide that?"

"Well, that's just being a woman on the internet," typed Eloise. "It's like a tire fire of misogyny on there. Even you, as a straight white male, if you ally yourself publicly with a woman and you go out of your way to treat her as a peer and an intellectual equal, I can almost guarantee that you'll start seeing men who will respect you less, because how dare you pretend that you're equal to a woman."

"I don't know what my definition of masculinity is, but it probably doesn't include 'feeling threatened by women,'" I typed.

"Being a woman today feels like," typed Eloise, "you're smart, you're sexually liberated, you're assertive, you have a strong sense of identity, and everyone hates you for it."

05

Emailing résumés and filling out job applications was kind of like watching internet porn, in that after a while I just felt disgusting, needed a break.

06

Scrolling through social media, I began to feel overwhelmed by the sheer amount of information at my disposal. I felt like

I was some sort of spy agency funded by the government, one whose sole purpose was to accumulate data about everyone and everything. I felt like I was the NSA. I felt like I was a bored version of the NSA.

Closing Google Chrome, I tried working on things for about an hour, which didn't go anywhere. I gave up, masturbated to internet porn and then browsed my life away again, first watching a video on Twitch of an expert player performing a flawless speed run of *Mega Man X2*, then discovering a Tumblr called *Glitch News*, which documented interesting glitches during real-life television news broadcasts.

Later, I went to the kitchen to make green tea. While waiting for the kettle, I examined Dana's bookshelf in the living room. Though Dana hadn't said anything to me about spirituality, her bookshelf contained many books about Eastern philosophy and Zen Buddhism. I picked out a book at random and began reading little passages. "During a meditation retreat," one passage said, "a student asked Soen Nakagawa, 'I am very discouraged. What should I do?' and Nakagawa replied, 'Encourage others.'"

This struck me as good life advice, so I decided to send a text message to Jane.

07

It was becoming increasingly obvious that my usual strategy of walking everywhere to save money wouldn't be compatible with Toronto. To compensate, I had begun experimenting with the city's public transportation system by avoiding paying fares in full. For whatever reason, Toronto's buses and trains weren't equipped with electronic change counters, making it easy to only put in whatever change you had on you, a kind of pay-what-you-can pricing model.

After riding the subway for 85 cents, I entered the gallery space of an artist-run centre to attend an opening that featured "technology-assisted paintings" and "passively interactive installations." Though the setting was familiar, I didn't recognize any of the faces in the crowd. I felt like I was in Montreal, except this was several years in the future and a new generation of generic artists and art students had taken over, replacing everyone I knew.

Standing alone amongst a group of strangers, my anxiety began to feel octopus-like, its arms reaching in every direction. "This is bad," I thought. "I need to find a new way to feel comfortable around people that doesn't involve alcohol." "What would make me feel more comfortable right now?" I thought, then pictured the gold medal I had won playing soccer as a child, the one I had stashed in a box in Grace's basement. I imagined myself wearing the medal in public, feeling confident and proud, the award around my neck impressing people around me.

Behind me, a girl wearing a jeans jacket kept saying the word "normative" while the person she was talking to kept saying "capital." "Normative capital," I thought. I pretended to look at an installation, then pretended to look at my phone, then ran out of things to pretend. I made fun of myself for mechanically drinking green tea while failing to interact with anyone. I had been spending so much time alone that I seemed to be feeling mostly numb looking at art, as if I had developed emotional arthritis. "I feel like a robot," I thought. "Or not even a robot, a drone. An unmanned drone flying around this room, firing my boredom at people."

I moved to the other side of the room to examine a painting that had been created using several algorithms, each set of instructions adding a new randomized layer of paint. One way to interpret these pieces, I thought, was as a representation of technology itself, how technology didn't exist in our lives as a united, continuous entity, but as different layers of noise that we constantly had to harmonize.

Inspecting the painting, I began to think about my own art, about what I was really trying to accomplish with glitches. I didn't view glitches as flaws, but as special occurrences. To me, every glitch was a unicorn. What I wanted, I thought, was to capture a glitch that could make you feel less alone, a glitch you could enter, a glitch that encompassed within it all of time, space and consciousness, the same way a drop of water can sometimes feel as if it contains the entire universe.

08

An hour and a half later, I sat on my bed and peered into Grace's bedroom through Skype. Behind her, I could see Tom-Tom licking himself, trying half-heartedly to clean his black fur coat, then giving up.

"I told Dom I would be taking the last weekend of August off to visit you and he flipped out at me," said Grace. "I don't know what's going on in his personal life, but everything has been making him explode lately. It's like he's a Michael Bay movie."

"He's good at being angry," I said. "He should be a wrestler on television."

"It's not even good anger," said Grace. "It's sad anger. He's just disappointed that his life is his life."

"Maybe that's how all wrestlers feel on the inside," I said, vaguely trying to be philosophical.

"Did I tell you that I signed up for my physics class?" said

Grace. "It's the last course I need as a prerequisite. After that, I'll be able to apply to physical therapy."

"So you would be starting physical therapy next year?" I said.

"If I pass physics and get accepted in the program, yes," said Grace. "I am a little nervous about physics because it's supposed to be hard, but we'll see how it goes. How's your job hunt going?"

"So-so," I said. "The job ads are all like, 'We're looking for a talented, driven self-starter' or something. I keep thinking, 'If I am a talented, driven self-starter, why would I start your company for you?'"

"Right," said Grace. "You would just start your own thing."

"Exactly," I said. "I feel tempted to send them my critique of their ad instead of a résumé. Maybe they would be impressed. Give me an interview."

09

I felt like my bank account was about to stage an intervention. It was the middle of August and I was running out of money, surviving by living like an insect, eating nothing but tofu, peanut butter, ramen noodles, dollar store ketchup, bread or rice that I "borrowed" from a giant container that belonged to Dana, hoping she wouldn't notice.

I started feeling jealous a little of my cat's food, which contained "many nutrients," "lots of proteins" and "antioxidants," according to the packaging.

Trying to make money quickly, I participated in a few "design competitions" on 99designs, an open platform that allowed graphic designers from all over the world to compete with one another for freelance contracts. Later, I successfully pitched a 900-word review of the technology exhibit to an art publication, which agreed to pay me $50, and secured a simple freelancing contract for a local animal hospital by aggressively underbidding everyone else, agreeing to do the work for almost nothing. Then I mass-emailed local bands to offer my services as a designer and received a response from an indie rock group who wanted me to create a music video for them using "3D effects and glitches." Their budget was $80, plus "free beers at one of our shows."

"That sounds great," I wrote back. I was exaggerating. It didn't sound that great.

Two days went by. Refreshing my inbox, I saw that I had received an email about an interview for a job at a water-heater company. I had replied to so many job ads that I couldn't remember which position this was for, or why I would have sent my resumé to a water heater company in the first place. "It was probably a generic office position," I thought.

"I can do that, I can do generic office work," I thought.

"Professional generic office worker," I thought.

The following morning, I sat on a black plastic chair in the sterile lobby of a small office located next to a gym on the second floor of an unassuming building on Yonge Street. I hadn't been up at 9 a.m. in a long time and it felt like my eyeballs were struggling to stay afloat in the blood pool of my skull. While waiting, I began flipping through the pamphlet about company values that the male receptionist had handed me. "It's the possibility of making your dreams come true that makes life interesting," read a sentence from the pamphlet. "Wait, are they expecting selling water heaters to be my lifelong dream?" I thought.

I wasn't sure why this would be anyone's dream.

"Do you play foosball?" said the male receptionist, trying to be friendly.

"Not really," I said.

"Oh," said the receptionist. "Well, I was just going to say that we have a foosball table. I am the office champion."

"Congratulations," I said, before realizing I was being sincere. Becoming office foosball champion seemed like a better lifelong dream to me than selling water heaters.

"Thank you," the receptionist said.

A few minutes passed. A woman with a heavy accent, who introduced herself as "Roxana" and then immediately explained that she was originally from Romania, came to greet me. "I am surprised you would want to do this, considering your background," Roxana said several minutes later, evaluating my résumé. I didn't think it was strange that I was interested in a generic office position, but I replied that I "loved new experiences" and that I "liked understanding how things around me functioned, like water heaters." I was obviously lying, but Roxana seemed to appreciate that I was willing to make the effort of lying outrageously about my identity and goals in life to secure this position.

I was asked to come back around 1 p.m. for a second interview.

Several hours later, I sat in a conference room next to two young men wearing dress shirts they didn't seem comfortable in. They had similar physical features, both jock-like and sporting a shaved head, though one had an earring while the other one didn't.

"Clones," I thought.

Roxana introduced us to the type of products the company offered, drawing on a whiteboard behind her as she went on. As she was listing the individual characteristics of three separate models of water heaters, I began second-guessing my decision to show up for this interview. I had no interest in learning about water heaters, felt so out of my comfort zone that my comfort zone was starting to seem like some sort of beautiful fantasy to me.

Next to me, the clones were smiling, trying too hard to be likeable, faking enthusiasm or asking forced questions to appear motivated and personally invested in the products.

"With our rental program, all repairs are free!" said Roxana, faking enthusiasm herself. "It's guaranteed."

"Wow," the clone with an earring said, which made me think of Roberto.

Without warning, a man with spiked hair wearing a yellow shirt barged into the room, interrupting the presentation.

"Alright," said the man. "Hello all. My name is Silver. Yes, this is my real name, as amazing as that sounds. As Roxana has explained to you, you will be spending today shadowing one of our team leaders."

This was not something that Roxana had explained to us.

"As you know," said Silver, "we won't be hiring all of you, so you need to impress the team leaders today. Ask questions! Be dynamic! This is a tremendous opportunity for you all. Now, who here has the best attitude?"

I didn't move. I thought, "I would rather kill myself than have the best attitude right now."

"I have the best attitude, Sir," said the earring clone.

"I like that," said Silver. "What's your name, son?"

"TJ," said the clone, getting up to shake Silver's hand. "It's a pleasure to meet you."

"Okay," said Silver. "TJ, because you have the best attitude, you'll be with Melissa today. She's a joy to be around."

"That's me," said a young woman entering the room. "Your

name's TJ? Come with me."

"Good, next," said Silver. "Which one of you two is going with Rahi today?"

"I'll go," I said, surprising myself by participating. Rahi, who was sporting dreadlocks and a short beard, entered the room and shook my hand in a professional manner, like a car salesman. I followed him down a hall, then another, then, somewhat distressingly, through a door that led outside, and finally to a van parked on the side of the road in which four men were waiting, each wearing the same blue shirt featuring the logo of the water heater company. "Wait, what are we doing?" I thought. I climbed into the van and sat on the only seat available. "Maybe they have a second office located somewhere else and they're providing transport?" I thought.

"Okay, so the plan is, we'll go grab food from somewhere, and then we'll tackle today," Rahi said. "Sounds good?"

I said, "Sure," aloud, then began to think that maybe I hadn't interviewed for an office position after all, but instead for one that involved selling water heaters to customers directly. I thought about asking Rahi to drop me off on the side of the road and then realized that the van was already speeding down an unknown highway. I wasn't sure I would be able to find my way back.

"Oh my god," said the driver, whose name was Fred. He retrieved his phone and photographed the car ahead of ours.

"Don't take pictures while driving," said Rahi. "Fred has this weird fetish for average cars. A Toyota Corolla! Oh my god!"

"It's not weird," said Fred. "You just don't get it. I am a car connoisseur."

"It's a Toyota Corolla," said Rahi. "If it was a Lamborghini, or at least a decked-out Corolla, then maybe. But a standard Corolla? There are a million of these. There's no point."

"You don't know anything," said Fred. "If you're telling me that you can't appreciate a fine car made for the modern man, then you're blind."

"Whatever," said Rahi.

The guys laughed. The group conversation shifted to playing *Call of Duty* online, with Rahi mentioning that playing video games before going to bed sometimes caused him to have dreams that felt "multiplayer," as if more than one person was logged into the dream and participating in real time, with "little to no lag."

About fifteen minutes later, we entered the parking lot of a mall.

"Watch this, guys," said Fred. "I am going to go all *Fast & Furious* on this parking spot."

"Don't," said Rahi, which didn't prevent Fred from parking the van somewhat recklessly, and succeeding at doing so.

"See," said Fred. "Wasn't that awesome?"

"I hate you," said Rahi. "Alright, everyone out."

Exiting the van, I followed the group inside the mall, then to a food court. The guys asked one another where they were going to eat and then all agreed that the person who had said "Taco Bell" had the best answer. Examining my surroundings, I spotted a sign indicating a subway station nearby. "Oh good, I can make my way back if I ditch them," I thought. I told Rahi that I was going to buy a sandwich and walked away. Once I was out of sight, I sat on a bench and used my phone to look up my current location on Google Maps.

"Daniel," said Rahi a few minutes later, suddenly behind me. "Are you getting food?"

"Yeah," I said. "I mean, no. To be honest, this isn't going to work for me. You guys seem nice, so it's nothing personal.

It's just, I hate this."

I thought about adding, "In a good way" to avoid insulting Rahi. "I hate this, but in a good way."

"Oh," said Rahi. "Well, what do you mean, you hate this?"

"There was no indication that this was a field position," I said. "Or maybe there was. I actually thought this was an office position, which already sounded pretty bad. I have no interest in doing door-to-door stuff."

"Well, it's not exactly door-to-door," said Rahi.

"Look, I don't want to waste your time. I saw a sign for a subway station nearby, so I think I'll just go," I said.

"Fine," said Rahi. "It's your call. The entrance to the subway station is that way, just outside the mall."

"Thank you," I said.

"Whatever," said Rahi.

10

"You just left?" said Grace on Skype, visibly unhappy with me. "Why would you leave? You need money."

"I couldn't do it," I said. "I couldn't fake being interested. There has to be a way for me to make money that doesn't involve being insincere, where I am not just putting up with a job because it gives me money to put up with it."

"But that's how it works in the real world," said Grace. "In the real world, you get a job and you do it and then you pay your rent. Do you think I like working in a pub? Well, sometimes I do, but I mean, my point is, I just get it over with and then I can do other things."

"I know that," I said. "It's not that I don't want a job. It's that I don't want a stupid job."

"I am not lending you money if you can't make rent," said Grace.

"I never asked you to do that," I said.

11

"Jobs are a place where you have to lie about having a personality to get money," Eloise typed on Facebook Chat.

12

Reading one of Dana's books about Zen Buddhism, I stumbled on a passage describing a concept called "the Original Face," which seemed to refer to the face you had before you were born, before your parents were born, back when you were nothing. Sitting on my bed, I tried to visualize my "original face," but couldn't picture what "nothing" looked like. All I could see was the colour black, with my thoughts reverberating inside my head like a gong.

13

I interviewed for two different jobs on the same day, both entry-level graphic design positions I was more than qualified to handle. Later, I was informed that neither interview would lead to a job offer. I wasn't sure where my applications had failed. I thought I had made a good impression during the meetings, plus had a solid résumé with years of experience on it. Before imploding and deciding to go freelance to pursue art full-time, I had worked in offices of various sizes for a few years. "Maybe they googled me and saw that *Vice* article and then automatically concluded that I am terrible because one crazy person on the internet seems to think that," I thought. I began to wonder if I would have to legally change my name to find employment. "Maybe that's the world we live in now," I thought. "You have to legally change your name every couple of years to prevent Google from fucking you over."

14

After spending the day staring at my laptop, I convinced myself to go out and attend a screening of videos by an internet artist named Jennifer Chan, who divided her time between Toronto and Chicago. On the way there, I thought about how I liked being alone too much. "I think I need fewer images and more real people in my life," I thought. "I need to go on some sort of image diet," I thought. "What does it mean to live your life primarily around images instead of people?" I thought.

"Me and my images," I thought.

It was Saturday night and only six days before Grace's visit to Toronto. The independent gallery in Kensington Market was decorated with old, broken television sets and hyperactive posters. I sat on a chair in the back row and watched everyone around me socialize.

Someone said, "Net art made the art world question its assumptions."

Someone said, "In the future, we'll look back on net art as just a transition."

Someone name-dropped the art collective Jodi.

Once again, I was alone in public and hiding inside what felt like a fort made out of my own anxiety, a kind of secret club for my problems and me. I glanced at the bar, was tempted to purchase and quickly drink a beer, but didn't want to end the hiatus, and also couldn't afford it. "Why am I even uncomfortable right now?" I thought. Though I usually blamed my social anxiety on the acne problems that had sabotaged my teenage years, I began to wonder if maybe something else was causing these issues, an imprint from even earlier in life, something to do with power and being too willing to adopt submissive stances.

Studying people around me, I started focusing on a person who reminded me a little of Evil Cayla. "Maybe she's the Evil Cayla of Toronto," I thought. She was chatting with a well-dressed man, who I decided to refer to in my head as "the Derek of Toronto." Labelling the pair in this manner made them seem more approachable, like I was role-playing to trick myself into thinking of them as potential friends, as opposed to unknowable strangers.

About ten minutes passed. An organizer thanked everyone for coming and introduced the first half of the screening. In a video projected onto a wall, two young men debated on Skype whether it was physically possible or not for an orca to leap over a seawall, as depicted in the final scene of the movie *Free Willy*. More videos were played, then a break, then videos again, then clapping.

After the screening, I stood outside and looked at the sky, which was moonless and uneven, a kind of patchwork of every cloud available on short notice. Behind me were Toronto Cayla and Toronto Derek, who was ranting about a guy he was seeing who always and only replied the letter "к" to his text messages, regardless of context. "It drives me nuts," Toronto Derek said.

Listening to his rant, I vaguely imagined myself inheriting from him the shirt he was wearing.

A few minutes later, Toronto Derek went back inside, leaving me alone with Toronto Cayla. I decided to force myself to talk to at least one person, found a way to get into a conversation with her simply by asking her what time it was, even though I had my phone on me. Toronto Cayla, whose real name was Michelle, asked me what had brought me to the screening, so I talked about having just moved here from Montreal and then my art practice, describing myself in a way that made me sound more successful than I actually was. One perk of being an artist was that you could be broke and unemployed, but still have self-esteem, sort of. Michelle didn't seem particularly impressed by my accomplishments. Though she was polite to me, she was also a little more distant and reserved than what I was accustomed to, masking her opinion of me instead of expressing it outwardly. I felt like I wasn't dealing with her directly, but as if she had re-directed me to her customer support service.

"Oh, wait, I think I read your name somewhere recently," Michelle said. "There was this *Vice* article about Montreal. Were you in that?"

"Yeah, I was in that," I said.

"You could sue for defamation for something like this, you know," she said. "I would. You should talk to a lawyer."

"I know a good lawyer," I said before realizing I was thinking of Cal, Elliot's bandmate, who was only a pretend lawyer.

"You said you just moved here from Montreal?" said Michelle. "I've been meaning to go there for a weekend, I just can't find the time. I heard that in Montreal, brunch lasts until 4 p.m."

We began comparing Montreal and Toronto, which was a conversation I had had on many different occasions in the past. As cities, Montreal and Toronto often seemed to function as fantasies for one another. People in Toronto usually perceived Montreal as a fun, inexpensive playground, a city that had, some-

90

how, outlawed responsibilities. Meanwhile, living in Montreal, it was easy to view Toronto as a city of grim productivity and career opportunities, the perfect environment in which to rediscover your inner adult. You moved to Montreal to have fun, you moved to Toronto to get your shit together. In reality, neither city was exactly that, though it was probably easier to discuss them in those terms.

15

"Sweater World," I thought, reading in my head the name of a small store across the street from me. "Head of social media at Sweater World," I thought, imagining myself working there. I was getting desperate for a job, but also tired of scanning job websites and emailing endless copies of my résumé to strangers. "I feel like every single person in Toronto has a copy of my résumé," I thought. I wanted a completely different system to find employment, maybe something like in a *Final Fantasy* video game where all you have to do to switch careers is put on a new hat, and your options include jobs like Red Mage or Monk.

16

Found a pair of cheap headphones abandoned at a café and then wondered if I could use them as a currency to pay my rent.

17

Logging into Facebook in the morning, I felt like some sort of indentured servant. "O Lord Facebook, I have come to pay tribute," I thought.

"Man-hating feminism feels like a dead end," read a sentence from an email from Jane.

19

Waiting for Grace outside the Ossington subway station, my attention was drawn to a man who was holding a dog with one hand and an iPhone with the other, trying, for some reason, to facilitate a conversation between the dog and the person on the other end of the call. It was a warm Friday evening and I could tell that a baby headache had hatched in a dark, humid corner of my brain. I was excited to see Grace, but also dreading having to show her how little I had accomplished on my own so far in Toronto.

A few minutes later, I saw her emerge from the crowd exiting the subway. "You're here," I said, hugging and kissing her.

"I am here," she said, smiling and mimicking my intonation. I offered to carry her backpack, which looked heavy, making me wonder if she had brought more things with her to spend one weekend in Toronto than I had to live here permanently.

"Thank you," said Grace. "My back is hurting."

"How was your Megabus?" I said.

"The ride was fine," said Grace. "We stopped in Kingston for a bit, but all I saw was a Tim Hortons and an empty parking lot, so it wasn't exactly a romantic getaway. What about you? What did you do today? Nothing, I am guessing."

"Not nothing," I said, annoyed a little. "Why would you say that? I am not just, like, sitting in the dark at home all day."

"Sorry," said Grace. "I wasn't trying to be mean. I just meant, you still don't have a job."

"It's been harder to find work than I thought it would be," I said. "I had two interviews last week and I thought they both went well, so I don't know what's not working. Maybe it's my résumé that's too complicated. I've done a lot of different stuff at this point, so it's hard to tell a story through my résumé that's straightforward and easy to understand."

"Your Twitter might be scaring them off," said Grace.

"I put it on private, though I am kind of getting tired of having to hide my online life when I am applying for jobs," I said. "It's like having split personalities, Corporate Me and Normal Me. Is it really a problem that I express bleak thoughts on Twitter? What does that have to do with anything?"

"Do you have any more interviews lined up?" said Grace.

"Just one, on Monday," I said. "I think it's a call centre. The job ad didn't say it was a call centre, but it sounds like that's what it is."

"If you're desperate, I guess it's not the worst thing in the world," said Grace. "You can do that for a little while and then quit. At least it's something. I can't believe you walked away from that water heater job when you're desperate for money, though."

"I still think that was a good decision," I said.

We boarded a bus, then sat next to one another near the entrance. Behind us, a man about my age, who was wearing sports sunglasses and a Chance the Rapper t-shirt, was listening to what seemed to be soft indie pop, with the lyrics of the song coming out of his headphones sounding something like, "Tell my dreams to give me up."

"Would you want to get beer tonight?" said Grace.

"I am still doing the hiatus, but you can drink if you want," I said. "We can stop at the LCBO."

"Oh, right," said Grace. "You can't buy alcohol in convenience stores here."

"Yeah, and apparently the LCBO closes at 9 p.m., which means you have to pre-plan how much alcohol you want and buy it before then," I said. "I don't understand how people put up with this. It feels like there should be massive riots against the LCBO or something. Led by Rob Ford."

"Rob Ford," said Grace. "So Toronto has this crazy party mayor, but getting drunk is impossible?"

"That's pretty much the gist of it," I said.

About ten minutes passed. Arriving at my apartment, I gave Grace a tour, which didn't take too long. "Battle!" said Grace, spotting my cat, who was sleeping in a moon chair. "Do you remember me, little lion? I am going to pretend that she remembers me."

After moving Grace's things to my room, I showed her Dana's pet chinchilla. The animal was patrolling its cage, looked overly anxious and apprehensive, like he was feeling heavily misunderstood.

"Is he really watching *Star Trek*?" said Grace, pointing out a computer monitor playing a DVD on loop. "Wait, it's a 'he,' right?"

"It's a he," I said. "Yeah, he likes watching television. Dana was telling me that it stimulates him mentally."

"I didn't know chinchillas did that," said Grace. "His eyes are crazy. It's like I am afraid of him, but I also want to pet him at the same time."

"Try petting him through the cage," I said. "He's alright, he just has trust issues."

"It's okay, little guy," said Grace. "We're all afraid of everything. Here, have space food."

She fed the chinchilla a dried raisin.

"I should get him *Star Trek* props for his cage," said Grace, "like a teleporter or a spaceship desk. Maybe he would like me more."

"That would be good," I said. "You could hire the guy who plays Spock to give him a dust bath."

Grace laughed. Returning to my room a few minutes later, she unzipped her backpack and retrieved two plastic binders. "Here, this is what you wanted, right?" she said.

"Yes, that's exactly it," I said. "Thank you for these."

"No problem," said Grace, smiling.

As a favour, I had asked her to bring me two binders I had stored in a box in her basement. The binders contained a full set of hockey cards that I had collected as a child, plus cards from a fantasy game called *Wyvern*, a failed *Magic: The Gathering* clone from the '90s.

"Are you really going to try selling your old hockey cards for money?" said Grace.

"Maybe," I said. "That doesn't seem more ridiculous to me than working for a water heater company."

"I guess not," said Grace.

We sat on my bed and talked for a long time. I asked Grace how Ashlyn and Roberto were doing and Grace said, "You love Roberto," and smiled and I replied, "Maybe I do." Several sentences later, Grace mentioned Dom, her manager at work who loved delivering bad news to people. All week, Grace had felt scared that Dom would tell her that she was being scheduled for a shift at the last minute for the sole purpose of preventing her from coming to visit me.

"Speaking of bad news," said Grace, "I should tell you that I am on my period."

She pouted in an overly exaggerated manner, expressing a

kind of cartoonish disappointment.

"I know this sucks, but there's a chance it might be over before I leave," said Grace. "There's hope!"

"It's fine," I said. "I mean, I'd love to have sex with you, but we can wait. I am okay with you being on your period. I love your period. I probably worship your period."

"What do you mean?" said Grace. "You like it when I am in pain?"

"No, I just mean, if you're on your period, then that means I didn't get you pregnant by accident," I said.

"I agree it wouldn't be good timing if I got pregnant," said Grace. "I'd like to at least be finally done with school before popping out a kid, although sometimes I wonder if I would just go for it if I got pregnant by accident. I don't know how many opportunities I'll have. Plus, getting an abortion is not, like, renting a movie and then returning it. You have a growing, living thing inside you and then you decide to cut it out. That shit is traumatic. It stays with you."

I wasn't sure what to say, so I replied, "Yeah," and nodded. Grace apologized again for being on her period.

"Don't be sorry," I said. "I am just glad you're here. I missed you. I missed your body. I feel like I forgot that you have a body."

"Well, I am glad you like my body," said Grace. "I like your body. We're both sexy."

"My body's not sexy," I said. "Your body is sexy. My body is just, like, there."

Grace laughed a little.

"I like how you don't make me feel bad about my flaws," she said.

"Like what?" I said.

"Like my thighs," said Grace. "Look at these things. They're a little big."

"Thank god for your flaws," I said. "It's way better for me if you're a real person and not, like, a supermodel or something. I don't even know what I would do with that."

Grace wanted to say something, but she stopped mid-sentence and added, "Sorry, hold on."

"Are you crying?" I said. "Why are you crying?"

"I don't know, I am just being emotional and retarded as usual," said Grace, laughing at herself. "Do you remember when we talked about my dad repeatedly telling me that no one was ever going to love me? That's such an awful thing to say to a child, but for a long time, I pretty much believed him. My boyfriends would be assholes to me and I would think, 'Well, that makes sense.' You have your issues, but all my friends like you, you're nice to me, like you bring me cupcakes from art shows and you offer to carry my bag without me having to ask, and I don't think you're a jerk. It sounds simple, but it's been honestly impossible for me to meet someone like that. I skyped with my dad last week and we talked about you. He wanted me to bring you with me to Newfoundland for Christmas."

"Would you want me to?" I said. "Come with you for the holidays, I mean."

"I'd be so happy if you came," said Grace. "Find a job. Just find any job so that you can buy a plane ticket to Newfoundland and meet my family."

"Newfoundland," I said.

20

On our way to Hub Coffee, Grace mentioned that she felt like her brain was "falling apart." The night before, just before going to bed, she had realized that she had forgotten her weed in Montreal, preventing her from following her usual routine. As a result, she hadn't slept very well, or at all.

"What did you do all night if you weren't sleeping?" I said.

"For a while, I just watched you fall asleep," said Grace. "I kept thinking, 'Don't fall asleep. Who's going to love me if you're asleep? Stay up and love me. Drink coffee if you have to.' I was just being silly."

"What did I do?" I said.

"You hid from me under the blankets in your sleep," said Grace.

"Oh," I said. "Sorry."

"It's okay, it's just funny," said Grace. "I actually got up at one point and tried working on my physics assignment, but I think I am ready to give up on that."

"I thought you just started physics," I said.

"I did, but I feel like I am in way over my head," said Grace. "The teacher is this tiny old man who mumbles a lot, and everyone around me look like they want to become real scientists who design spaceships or create invincible babies. I just need this course to apply to physical therapy. I keep thinking that I don't belong there at all."

"I didn't realize it was that bad," I said. "What if you got tutored or something?"

"You don't understand," said Grace. "It's hard for me to concentrate on something like physics. I really think I have undiagnosed ADHD. So far, I've been able to get by with Dexedrine that I purchase from Derek from time to time, but it's not enough for this. I've been trying for months to motivate myself to get up early in the morning, go to the walk-in clinic at the hospital and get my blood work done so that I can get a proper Adderall prescription, but I kept putting it off and now it's killing me."

"Do you think weed is preventing you from going?" I said. "Like, it's draining your willpower?"

"It can't be," said Grace. "It's not like I smoke that much. Only to fall asleep. And when I need to chill. Or when I am with people."

We entered Hub Coffee and began waiting in line, then Grace ordered a latte and a baked treat. She offered to buy me tea, but I didn't want her to spend money on me, so I replied that I was happy with just a glass of water. "You can have a piece of my cookie if you want," Grace added. As we waited for her beverage, she started chatting with an employee. Within a few sentences, she was laughing with him and seemed to have befriended him. "Oh right, she's good at talking," I thought. I felt impressed by her ability to connect with strangers so effortlessly, and it suddenly seemed odd to me that I was the one with thousands of friends on social media when she was clearly so much better at interacting with people than I ever would be.

Grace found a way to include me in the conversation and we had a nice, friendly chat with the café employee. I thought about how I wasn't exactly the same person when I was with Grace, how her presence had a kind of normalizing effect on me, the same way the moon stabilizes the Earth's rotation. It seemed obvious that I made better decisions, was a much saner person overall with her around.

Back outside about twenty minutes later, Grace noticed a red bicycle locked to a pole across the street. "My bike!" she shouted. "This is so random. It looks exactly like the bike Michael stole from me."

"Could you imagine if this was actually your bike?" I said.

"It's probably not, but I told you that Michael is cray-cray,

99

right?" said Grace. "I picture him doing something like this, bringing my bike all the way to Toronto and leaving it here just to be an asshole to me and, I don't know. It doesn't seem unreasonable. It sounds like something he would do."

"If we go to Newfoundland, we should throw a party where we invite all your ex-boyfriends," I said.

"Oh god," said Grace, laughing nervously. "You don't want that."

21

On our way to a public park, we decided to stop to examine a selection of used books that a man was selling on a street corner. I flipped through a book titled *Megatrends 2010*, then asked Grace what she was looking at and she showed me a copy of *The Shipping News*, a novel set in Newfoundland that had been adapted into a movie starring Kevin Spacey.

"It'd be funny to watch it," I said.

"The movie version?" said Grace. "I've never seen it. A while ago, someone told me it portrayed Newfoundlanders as idiots, so that's why I've never bothered."

"I just want to have some idea of what to expect from Newfoundland," I said.

"Well, that movie wouldn't be a realistic representation, but I guess we could try watching it," said Grace.

"What should I know about Newfoundland?" I said.

"Let's see," said Grace. "Dad is going to want to screech you in for sure. It's this tradition in Newfoundland. Anyone who isn't from the island has to get screeched in and become an honorary Newfie. You might have to kiss a fish."

"Is your family going to want to take me hunting or something?" I said. "You should tell them that I don't know anything about nature or surviving."

"Dad isn't much of a hunter, so I don't think you have to worry about that," said Grace. "He might talk to you about going for fish and chips. He loves fish and chips."

"I can pretend I love fish and chips," I said.

About ten minutes passed. At the park, we sat on a patch of grass and observed people around us. Grace began massaging her right foot, which sometimes caused her discomfort.

"Who are all these people?" I said.

"They're just people," said Grace.

"Like, who is that guy?" I said, pointing out a white man sporting a visor who was walking two dogs while rollerblading. "What is he doing here? Why does he have two dogs? Do we need him? He seems redundant. It doesn't seem like we need him at all."

"What do you mean?" said Grace. "He just lives here."

"I know," I said. "I think what I am trying to say is, sometimes it feels like we have way too many humans. It's not funny anymore. That's why one of the best things you can do for the environment is not reproduce. People who don't have children are usually called 'selfish,' but I don't know if that's true anymore. Maybe the unselfish thing to do now is to not have babies."

"If the world really goes to shit, we could just move to Newfoundland," said Grace. "Newfoundland is cold now, but maybe it will be awesome by then."

22

In the living room, Dana's pet chinchilla was rolling around in his plastic ball and looking confused, like a 2D character trying to navigate a 3D environment. I introduced Grace to Dana, who was quietly working on a 3,000-piece puzzle in the living room. Grace and I moved to the kitchen, where we made chickpea curry for dinner.

"Do you want to watch *MasterChef* while we eat?" I said.

"You're asking me if I want to watch *MasterChef*?" said Grace. "You don't even like *MasterChef*."

"I think I am starting to be weirdly okay with it," I said. "I found something that I like about it. *MasterChef* isn't really a show about food, it's a show about work. It's about what we want work to feel like. When you work in an office, you rarely get clear feedback or feel like you're being pushed to explore the full limits of your talents. You can phone it in and it doesn't make that much of a difference. With *MasterChef*, they take these random people and then they challenge them to make the best food they've ever made in insane conditions. When the contestants manage to surpass themselves and actually create something good under pressure, it's almost like they attain this kind of beautiful nirvana."

Later, we sat side by side on my bed and watched an episode on my laptop. While Gordon Ramsay was yelling at someone, I got up and went to the kitchen to make green tea. I returned holding a teapot filled with hot water, then lost my balance because of my cat, who startled me by running through my legs. I tripped and spilled most of the teapot's content onto my MacBook and left thigh. The laptop emitted a loud wail, what sounded like a computer's version of agony, then shut down. Grace got up quickly from the bed and said, "Oh my god, are you okay?" and I replied that I didn't care about my leg, was more concerned about the computer.

"Fuck," I said. "That's such a stupid accident."

"Don't freak out," said Grace, placing my MacBook upside down on a pillow. "Maybe it's not that bad. Maybe your computer will be okay once it's had time to chill and dry out. Just seal it in a bag of rice and don't touch it for a few days."

"It's fucked," I said. "I just know it's fucked. Shit."

"Relax," said Grace.

"I can't, just, not have a computer," I said. I tried to imagine living my life without a computer, and it felt the same as trying to imagine living without a central nervous system.

"Leave your computer alone for a few days and then you can re-assess," said Grace. "You can use my computer while I am here. I'll give you the password to my MacBook. After that, maybe you can use a public computer at a library or something like that."

"Fuck," I said. "Fuck, fuck, fuck."

"I don't think I've ever seen you this upset," said Grace.

23

On Monday morning, I rode the subway with Grace, who was accompanying me to my job interview, her bus back to Montreal scheduled for later that afternoon. A man standing near us was wearing a t-shirt that featured the logo of the Satanic Temple, so Grace and I ended up talking about the organization and I mentioned that I thought their political activism in the u.s. was great.

"That was a good weekend," said Grace, changing the conversation topic. "Well, except for your MacBook. Is your leg okay?"

"I'll be fine," I said. "It's just a minor burn. Maybe I should come visit you next month. I don't know with what money, but I can figure something out."

"That would be nice," said Grace. "In the meantime, you'll get a break from all my yapping."

"But I like your yapping," I said.

"That's not true," said Grace. "When I get really chatty, you just tune me out now. It's okay. I am not mad or anything. I would tune me out, too."

"If I do, I don't mean to tune you out," I said.

"It's fine," said Grace. "I get it."

Exiting the subway, we walked for a few minutes until we reached the correct building. I pressed the elevator call button and Grace said, "Good luck," then left to go check out a health food store across the street. I rode the elevator, introduced myself to a receptionist, then sat in a waiting room. During my interview, I impressed a short, pudgy man with a Spanish accent by pretending I had a good attitude and giving socially acceptable reasons to explain why I was interested in this position. The pudgy man asked me if I was bilingual and I replied that I could speak broken French, so he wrote "Intermediate" on my file. Later, I was interviewed a second time by an HR representative and then offered a position on the spot. I signed an employment contract and the HR representative smiled and shook my hand and said, "Welcome aboard," and I imagined moving a cursor over his face and selecting "Force Quit > Conversation."

"Please don't tell anyone I work in a call centre," I said to Grace, coming out.

24

The Apple Store felt more like a public pool in the summertime than a business selling consumer electronics. It was several days later and I was watching employees in blue t-shirts run around, visibly struggling to keep up with demand. I wondered if anyone had ever developed PTSD from working in an Apple Store. I had my MacBook with me, though I felt like I already

ready knew what the Apple Store employee was going to tell me, that my MacBook was in a terrible condition, that my warranty didn't cover water damage, that repairing my laptop would cost more money than I had.

Three hours later, I sat on an office chair inside the call centre's training room, which featured beige walls, claustrophobic lighting, outdated training computers and ventilation pipes that looked like brass instruments. The room felt like a computer lab from the late '90s, the kind of retro aesthetics that reminded me of post-internet art. I was part of a group of twelve undergoing training, and everyone except a chirpy woman, who was carefully noting down the seven motivational keywords listed on the opening slide of a PowerPoint presentation, seemed glum and contemplative, as if everyone in the room was thinking, "This is a new low point in my life."

A man in his early thirties wearing a blazer and a plaid hat entered the room.

"Alright, so before I get the presentation underway, I'd like to talk about these keywords that you see onscreen right now," said the man, who was named Andre. "You see these? What are those? Why are they there?"

"To motivate us," said a young woman wearing a red cardigan.

"That's exactly it," said Andre, "and I have a very simple analogy to help you understand how to apply them. Do any of you watch *Breaking Bad*? Do you guys know that show?"

"I love that show," said someone sitting behind me.

"What is it?" said a man wearing a turtleneck. "I don't know what it is."

"It's this teacher who has cancer, and this hot guy, and they're selling drugs to cure the cancer," said the girl with the red cardigan.

The chirpy woman wrote down the words *Breaking Bad*.

"If you don't know what that is, look it up when you get home," said Andre. "It's an amazing TV show. Trust me. You'll thank me later."

Andre began describing at length the pilot episode of *Breaking Bad*, trying to relate in broad terms the main character's predicament to the motivational keywords onscreen and to our future responsibilities as call agents. "See that, see how that works?" Andre said, followed by a sustained grin. "Any questions?"

Checking my phone, I became aware that we had somehow spent forty-five minutes getting through the initial Power-Point slide.

Moving on, Andre introduced us to the insurance package we would be selling on behalf of one of the largest banks in Canada. "Have a little fun when speaking to customers!" read a sentence from the PowerPoint. "Accidental death insurance," read another. As the presentation progressed, it became obvious that the insurance package contained several complicated clauses that made it nearly impossible to redeem, meaning the package itself was more or less a con, a kind of useless product that existed not to fill a consumer need, but because the senior executives of a bank somewhere had decided that they needed more numbers in their numbers.

After the presentation and a short break, Andre announced to the group that it was time for a "team exercise." He assigned everyone a partner. I was paired with a man named Ohio, who was very tall and a former car salesman. During the opening presentation, Ohio had seemed largely uninterested, playing *Candy Crush Saga* on his phone while barely pretending to follow along, which had made me think positively of him.

"Default guy friend," I thought.

In groups of two, we were instructed to role-play the automated script that a call centre agent had to follow. One person would play the role of the calling agent, while the other would pretend to be a customer.

"Hello sir or madam, my name is Danny," I said, following the script. I was using "Danny" as my calling agent name, hoping that using a different name would make this less humiliating, as if this was happening to someone else. "I am calling on behalf of your bank. How are you today?"

"Good," said an indifferent Ohio.

"I am calling you today to tell you that you've been pre-approved for a free $2,000 accidental death insurance package," I said. "For $9.34 a month, you can get $100,000 in accidental death insurance, plus your complimentary $1,000, which is free."

"Okay," said Ohio. "Sign me up."

"You have to ask me more questions than that," I said. "No one would say 'Sign me up' right away. Just tell me that you need to talk about it with your spouse."

"Okay," said Ohio. "I have to talk about this with my spouse, but then sign me up."

On the training computer, I selected the "spouse" dialogue option and read the corresponding message, ad-libbing a little. In tone, the script felt emotionally manipulative, with frequent and seemingly gratuitous references to the consumer's "loved ones."

"Did you know that your spouse would also be covered by our insurance package?" I said. "You'll have peace of mind knowing your loved ones will be taken care of after your accidental death. Should we begin your enrollment now?"

"Okay," said Ohio, laughing. "Sign me up. This is dumb."

"Let's just get through this," I said. "At least they're paying us."

25

I completed the call centre's four-day training program and then worked two days on the floor. Sitting in my cubicle, waiting for the auto-dialer to compose a phone number on file, I thought about how I felt relieved that I hadn't made a single sale so far. "A least I don't have to feel guilty for selling someone magic beans," I thought.

In my headphones, a voice said, "Hello?" so I began reciting the automated script. The voice listened to me for a little while and then decided to hang up. I agreed with the voice that hanging up on me was the right decision.

"This is such a depressing waste of time," I thought. "This isn't my life. My life is going nowhere working on art stuff. How do I get back to my life?"

26

"You quit your job over email?" said an annoyed Grace on Skype. "Daniel, what the hell? How are you going to pay rent?"

27

Browsing the internet using an outdated computer in a pub-lic library, I thought about how I viewed jobs more or less like sugar daddies, how my approach in life was to try to manip-ulate society into giving me money so that I could afford to do art. "Shit, that's pretty much how a heroin addict lives," I thought. "Society is just something to take advantage of, nothing matters except finding money for your next hit."

"I am like an art junkie," I thought.

28

The same day my first and only paycheque from the call centre was deposited into my account, I found a buyer online for my collection of Wyvern cards. It was the second week of September. The cards, it turned out, didn't have much value at all, and the person who had agreed to purchase them from me wasn't even interested in them as a collectible, just wanted to be able to play the original game.

"I don't know what I was expecting," I thought. "Though $20 is $20, I guess."

I was already regretting my decision to quit the call centre, regretting going freelance, regretting ever getting into art. "If I had a steady job, I probably would have enough money to just order a new MacBook right now," I thought.

"Spilling water onto a laptop is all it takes for me to reconsider my entire life," I thought.

29

Reading quotes about the concept of "the Original Face" on my phone, I found one by a French philosopher named Gaston Bachelard that said, "How should one perform the image of nothing if not by exaggerating it?"

30

"What type of job are you looking for?" read a prompt above

the search engine of a job website.

"Anything," I typed on the library computer keyboard.

31

"Okay, I am here," read an unexpected Facebook message from Eloise. She had apparently travelled overnight from New York without warning me in advance that she was coming.

"Look at us," I said, meeting her a few hours later in front of Saving Gigi, a café on Bloor West. "Hanging out in real life."

"I know," said Eloise. She was smiling and wearing a black dress paired with an acrylic necklace in the shape of an eye. "I am as shocked as you are."

"It's good to see you," I said.

"You too," said Eloise.

We hadn't seen each other in person in about nine months, so I wasn't sure what to expect from her. The last time we had been in the same room at the same time, in Brooklyn on New Year's Eve, she had been dealing with emotional problems unrelated to me, had felt, at times, distant and forlorn and unreachable, like a dying star.

"I almost said, 'Long time no see,'" I said, "but then that's not true at all. I see you on Instagram all the time."

"This is so strange," said Eloise after a pause, then laughing.

"It makes sense that it's odd," I said. "I mean, we're so used to never hanging out in person. We're together now, but it feels like tomorrow we'll just go back to talking on Facebook like nothing happened."

"That sounds about right," said Eloise. "What do you think of Toronto so far?"

"It's good," I said. "My only problem is money, though that's probably my fault. I thought it would be easier to find a job I don't hate."

"Can't you get a job in a bar or a café or something?" said Eloise.

"I don't have any experience doing that," I said. "Though I guess I could try. I don't even have a computer right now, I spilled water onto mine and I don't have enough money to get it fixed."

"Wow, I didn't realize things were so dire," said Eloise. "I hope you figure something out. If it makes you feel better, my financial situation right now is just as awful. My problem is that I can't work legally in the u.s."

"We need a money-making scheme or a grant or something," I said.

"A few weeks ago, someone told me that if you get pregnant in Denmark, they just give you a bunch of money," said Eloise. "Maybe that's what we should do. Get pregnant in Denmark."

Eloise invited me to her friend Jessica's apartment, where she was staying for the weekend. I followed her through a series of perpendicular, increasingly residential streets, and then into a house that had been converted into individual apartments. The building's layout felt needlessly complicated, almost maze-like, as if it had been designed not by an architect but by a role-playing dungeon master. I imagined the house having a cool dungeon name, something like "The Tower of Chaos" or "The Dragon's Tomb."

We entered an apartment and sat in the kitchen.

"The Tower of Chaos' kitchen," I thought.

"I am so happy we have Moosehead," said Eloise, grabbing a bottle from the fridge and sounding disproportionately excited for what was basic Canadian beer. "It tastes terrible, I just haven't had it in a while."

"Moosehead," I said. "I wonder if anyone would drink this if it was named after any other part of the moose. Like Moose Liver."

"Moose Butt," said Eloise, opening her beer. "I would drink something called Moose Butt."

"Shit, you're right," I said. "Me too."

"Moose Butt," said Eloise. "Do you want a beer?"

"I am okay," I said. "I am actually doing a hiatus right now. I am not drinking or partying for a while."

"Really?" said Eloise. "So wait, if you don't have a computer and you haven't been drinking or partying, what have you been doing?"

"I have no idea," I said.

"Well, I'd offer you something else, but Jess only has beer and Gatorade," said Eloise. "Do you want Gatorade? It's blue."

"I am good, but thank you for offering," I said. "So how do you feel about being here?"

"It's fine," said Eloise. "When I was on the bus and I first saw the city in the distance, I briefly thought, 'I want to run away,' except then I realized, I already did that? I kept imagining coming back here and discovering that a copy of me has been here the whole time and that my friends like the copy better. Less drama."

"That's not true," shouted Jessica from another room. "We missed you."

"Thanks," said Eloise.

"I feel like you live both nowhere and everywhere right now," I said.

"It's an extreme lifestyle," said Eloise. "I thought the part of my life where I wander around Manhattan in the middle of the night was over, but apparently it's doing a comeback."

"So you're going back to New York on Monday?" I said.

"Yeah," said Eloise. "The whole New York thing started last year around New Year's, when you and I were both in Brooklyn. Then I came back, then there was Baltimore with Julie, and now I am trying to see how long I can stretch out this period of my life. The biggest issue is that since I don't have an American visa, I can only stay there for six months at a time. That's why I am here now. I just had to exit the u.s. for a few days, but I am going back as soon as possible."

I was hoping Eloise would tell me she was planning on moving back to Toronto soon, so this wasn't good news. I tried to hide my disappointment, but I could tell it had already blown up all over my face like bubble gum.

"You should move back and live in Roncesvalles with me," shouted Jessica from the other room.

"Jess is moving to Roncesvalles soon," said Eloise. "Her new apartment has a sun room."

I thought, "The Tower of Chaos doesn't have a sun room."

"Have you been working on anything new?" said Eloise. "I guess not, if you don't have a computer."

"I've been trying, but I feel like everything I make has been mediocre lately," I said. "I don't know what I am doing wrong or why it's not working anymore. Art in general just feels very empty to me all of a sudden. It's like, you upload a video online, people press the Like button, then they move on and the next day, nobody cares anymore. I feel good temporarily and then twelve hours later, everything is back to normal. Why am I doing this to myself again?"

"That's just social media, though," said Eloise. "That's what always happens."

"I don't know," I said. "It just seems weird that I try so hard not to have a job so that I can do the art thing, then I do the art thing and it feels more like a consolation prize than anything else. Maybe I am not talented enough to become anything. Maybe I am only talented enough to be talented."

"You're doing fine," said Eloise. "That's not you talking, that's the internet talking. Don't co-sign the internet's bullshit. You're only feeling insecure because of that *Vice* article."

"No, it's not that," I said. "I am fine with the *Vice* thing. It's more like, what if all I am doing with art is damaging my life? I really love being creative and working on new projects and stuff, but if I ever stop thinking of art as something meaningful in my life, I feel like I would have nothing left. It'd be like going bankrupt."

"Let me ask you this," said Eloise, "can you imagine yourself doing anything other than what you're doing now?"

"I don't know," I said. "Probably not."

"Then, there you go," said Eloise. "Life is hard, but keep going. Something good will happen. Just focus on what you have control over. You should show your work in a gallery here or something. I know people you could talk to."

"Thanks," I said. "I think I will eventually, but right now, I feel like I need to focus on my money situation."

"Right," said Eloise, opening a second beer. The conversation shifted to artists I knew tangentially from the internet who Eloise had met in person while living in New York and Baltimore. She told me a story about meeting a person we both followed on Twitter who was affiliated with the website Rhizome. At the party Eloise had attended, the person, wearing a white suit with NASCAR-like advertisements sewn onto it, had showed her an Instagram picture of himself and Marina

Abramovic both wearing what appeared to be early models of Oculus Rift virtual reality headsets.

"Meeting people I know from the internet in person is so much easier than meeting random strangers," I said. "Usually, we've already lurked one another online and pre-decided whether or not we're going to like each other."

"At this point, I am not even sure where I would go to meet non-internet people," said Eloise. "I guess, 'a bar' or something."

"'A bar,'" I said, copying her intonation. "That's funny. We should go to 'a bar' together."

"Oh lord, no," said Eloise. "When I was in Baltimore, some-one asked me, 'Are you online?' like this was 1998 and I was like, 'What? What do you mean?' It was so obvious to me that I constantly was."

32

"Where the fuck is Ken?" said Eloise. She was checking her phone regularly and her tone was playful, though with some frustration mixed in. It was the following night and we were waiting in Koreatown for Ken, an old friend of Eloise who had invited her to karaoke. Sitting on the sidewalk, I tried to determine whether or not "going to karaoke" would count as "partying," which would technically end my party hiatus.

It didn't count, I determined.

Sober karaoke didn't count as partying.

"Sorry I am late," said Ken about fifteen minutes later.

"It's okay," said Eloise. "I like the hair. Look at this."

"I've had this haircut for a while now," said Ken. "I think it's better."

"No, definitely," said Eloise, touching Ken's head a little and laughing.

Ken was wearing an orange polo and black sports shorts, was probably in his mid-twenties, didn't look at all like how I would have imagined Eloise's friends from high school.

"I am sorry I couldn't see you when you were in New York," said Eloise. "I was stuck in Baltimore."

"Oh, don't worry about it," said Ken. "It's funny, I was with Bryce and he kept saying, 'Oh, she won't make it in time because her friend was in an accident, how convenient.'"

"But Julie really was in an accident," said Eloise. "It was scary."

"No, I know," said Ken. "I didn't think you were lying. It just sounded too perfect."

"If I didn't want to see you, I would have told you that, and then the reason why," said Eloise.

"I wasn't accusing you of lying," said Ken. "Bryce was. Anyway, it doesn't matter. Look at us, we're arguing."

"It's true," said Eloise. "Sorry."

"It's okay," said Ken. "It took us about a minute to go from happy to arguing."

"We haven't lost it," said Eloise, laughing. She explained that she and Ken had dated a long time ago, though only for a brief period. "This was back when I still believed in men," she added.

We walked for about a minute and entered Freezone Karaoke. We descended the stairs leading to the basement and followed Ken into a private room inside which people were currently destroying "You Oughta Know" by Alanis Morissette. The room was decorated with faux leather couches, a karaoke machine, a disco ball, coloured lights, tambourines and wired microphones.

Ken said hello to everyone, opened a beer and immediately drank the top half.

"What should we sing?" said Eloise, who was already flipping through an encyclopedia of late '90s jams.

"Are we singing?" I said. "We just got here and it's their room. We can't just, like, take over."

"Who cares?" said Eloise. "Karaoke was invented to allow people to be rude. You can do whatever at karaoke. It's like having diplomatic immunity."

While Eloise was picking a song, I took out my phone and tried to take a photo of the room, but the picture came out blurry and low quality, as if it had been taken by a lunar module on a mission in outer space. "I should force myself to interact with people," I thought. I was feeling anxious by default, could sense a mental resistance inside me preventing me from feeling comfortable. "Partying while sober feels like a completely different universe," I thought. "It's like travelling to Narnia." I tried to isolate what, if anything, drinking alcohol in this situation would make different, and it dawned on me that maybe the only thing I liked about alcohol was that it altered my state of mind, which led to me acting or feeling different. "When I am drinking, my situation never changes, it's me that changes," I thought. "When I feel anxious around people, maybe all I need to do is change my perspective."

I decided to test this theory by forcing myself to do something out of character. I turned to Eloise, who was still flipping through the oversized songbook, and pointed at the first song title I recognized.

"This one," I said. "Can we sing this one?"

"You want to sing 'When 2 Become 1' by the Spice Girls?" said Eloise.

"Yes," I said. "Desperately."

"Wow, okay," said Eloise. "Sure."

Five songs later, our selection came up onscreen. Eloise and I grabbed microphones and began following the lyrics. We performed a touching rendition of the romantic ballad and I made the room laugh by singing the chorus with energy and over-the-top emotion. "I am doing it," I thought. "I am changing my perspective."

"I didn't know you had that in you," said Eloise as the song was ending.

"I can be a beast at karaoke," I said. "I just need to get into it."

Passing the microphone to someone else, I sat on a leather couch next to Ken, who asked me if I was enjoying Toronto so far. I wanted to say, "Toronto is hellish, in a good way," but then decided not to, simply replying, "Yeah," instead. I mentioned my job situation and Ken offered to introduce me to his friend Will, who owned a language school. "They're always looking for ESL teachers," Ken explained. "It's easy. You don't even need teaching experience."

About an hour and a half passed. Ken, now several beers in, performed a disorderly version of "Say It Ain't So" by Weezer. He was now slurring his words a little, his sentences becoming less and less coherent, containing only enough information to be somewhat decipherable, a kind of minimalism, like a child's drawing. Watching Ken, I thought about how, in the span of a few hours, he had gone from intelligent human being to drunken mess. Had I been drinking, I probably would have barely noticed this transformation, but since I was sober, it looked absolutely horrifying.

I left the private room to go to the bathroom. Coming out, I ran into Eloise, who asked me if I wanted to step outside.

"It's so hot in there," Eloise said about a minute later, sitting on the sidewalk in front of Freezone Karaoke. "I wanted to ask you, how's Grace? How's long distance going?"

"Grace is good," I said. "I honestly feel like I might be in one of the best relationships of my life right now."

"Aw, that's cute," said Eloise.

"I don't know if that's going to sound crazy, but one thing I like about Grace is that she's not a doomed artist," I said. "Before her, the last few people I was involved with were all artists who had insane egos because of the constant validation they get on social media."

"Right," said Eloise. "I hate how much of an echo chamber the internet has become. It's impossible to have any perspective. You're rarely as big of a deal as you think you are."

"My only concern with Grace is that I have no idea if I can give her what she wants long-term, which is not even that much," I said.

"Well, maybe you don't have to know just yet," said Eloise. "How old is she again?"

"Grace?" I said. "She's 32."

"Okay," said Eloise. "Well, you don't have to decide now, but you should probably be careful. Time is different when you're a woman. You only have so many eggs."

"I know," I said.

"I don't know why I was so afraid of coming back here," said Eloise. "This weekend was fine. Now that I am here, I almost wish I was staying an extra day."

"You should move back," I said.

"I am not sure I am ready," said Eloise, "but come visit me in New York if you can."

33

Alone in my room, I watched an entire episode of *MasterChef* on my phone by myself, then another, then another. "I miss you," I texted Grace.

34

"Something happened at the border," read a Facebook message from Eloise. "I got pulled aside. The border people didn't want me to re-enter the u.s. I told them I wasn't making money through art and they didn't believe me. They googled me. They said, 'You run this magazine, all these Brooklyn places are talking about you.' I said, 'I've been living on my savings.' They searched my bag and wallet and eventually they decided to let me go. They had to accept that sometimes there's no money in art. It looked troubling for them. It was funny."

35

Over email, Ken arranged for me to interview for a position as an ESL teacher at his friend Will's language school. The day of the interview, I sat on a chair in Will's office and observed him trying to multitask, talking on the phone while typing on a keyboard. He was wearing a plain shirt tucked into dark-grey pants, had a short mustache, round glasses. He seemed stressed and nervous in a way that reminded me of Dana's pet chinchilla.

I imagined feeding Will a dried raisin, to make him feel calmer.

"Right, sorry about that," said Will, ending his phone call. "So, I had a look at your résumé. Can you tell me a little bit more about you, about your past work experience?"

"I just moved here from Montreal," I said. "I am a freelance designer and artist. I don't have teaching experience, but I have done talks and presentations before. Freelancing is a bit of a roller coaster, so I'd love to find something more stable to complement it."

"What kind of clients do you have?" said Will.

"I just finished freelancing for one of the largest banks in Canada," I said.

"Okay," said Will. "Well, that's interesting. Let me tell you a little bit about how we do things around here. Our school uses a 'conversational' approach to teaching, which I think sets us apart. Most of our students are Korean, and what we do is, we pair each student with a native English speaker, to give them the chance to learn by talking. Not a lot of schools do that, because they're too focused on profits. They'll just hire one teacher for twenty people."

"So, all I have to do is chat with the students?" I said.

"It's a little more complicated than that, but essentially, yes," said Will. "You'll have conversations with them about the topic of the day, then you'll give them feedback on what they did well and what they could improve. The students usually have questions about words they didn't understand, so you'll have to answer those."

"That seems fine," I said.

Will asked me a few more questions, then mentioned he would be willing to give me a few shifts and see how it goes. "Paid to talk," I thought. "Grace's dream job," I thought. The next day, I returned for my first shift and was paired with another teacher, who was also named Daniel, as well as his current student, who introduced himself as "Teddy" before specifying that Teddy was his "American name."

"Was this," said Teddy before hesitating, "okay?"

"It was a great sentence," said the other Daniel. "Don't worry so much. You're doing great."

"I had no problem understanding you," I said. "You killed it."

"Killed it?" said Teddy.

121

"Actually, this is good vocabulary for you," said the other Daniel. "'Killing it' is an expression. It means you executed a particular task very well."

"Oh," said Teddy before writing down "Killing it" on a piece of paper.

About an hour passed. We helped Teddy prepare for a "group debate" on the topic of global warming, which involved all students in the class. When his name was called, Teddy stood in front of the class and argued that global warming was "bad" because "the world is important." Other students agreed with him. Teddy seemed pleased with himself.

"He's killing it," I thought.

36

"I would have never guessed that you would like being an ESL teacher," said Grace on Skype, "but hey, whatever works for you." It was the first week of October and I was finally making money again. In addition to teaching English, I was also giving web design lessons to some Korean students from the school outside of school hours. This was technically "frowned upon," but didn't seem to be enforced in any way.

"I am shocked I like it too," I said. "All I know is that it feels better than working in some bullshit office where I am not even sure I understand why my job exists in the first place."

"That makes sense," said Grace.

"How's physics going?" I said. "You haven't brought it up in a while."

"Well," said Grace before pausing. "I didn't want to tell you because I felt like a failure, but I actually dropped out three weeks ago. I was spending all my free time doing homework and even then, I couldn't keep up. The teacher would give us these pop quizzes in class and I would get scared that I was going to fuck up in school all over again and my brain would just freeze. It was like I had amnesia all of a sudden. I couldn't remember anything. There was no way in hell I would have passed that class."

"That's terrible," I said.

"Physics is just so damn hard," said Grace. "Biology I could do, but physics is just insane. I feel like I did too much MDMA in my big partying days and now my brain is broken. It doesn't help that whenever I struggle, I panic and think that I am never going to be anything more than a hostess in a pub."

"Get on Adderall," I said. "Get on Adderall and try again next semester. I'll help you. We'll find you a tutor or something."

"I can't believe I still haven't gone to get my blood work done," said Grace. "I am such a piece of shit. I need to stop being afraid that people at the hospital will only be speaking French to me."

"Is that all that's preventing you from going?" I said.

"Well, not all, but it's not helping," said Grace.

"You should have said something earlier," I said. "I didn't realize that this was making you feel anxious. Do you want me to come with you? I'll speak broken French to them. I don't care."

"You don't need to come with me," said Grace.

"I want to," I said.

37

A week later, I was finally able to get my MacBook repaired and began working at the Starbucks near the language school almost every day, like I was doing some sort of artist residency there.

I had missed my laptop so much that I ended up experiencing a powerful burst of manic productivity. After a few days of frantic work and editing, I uploaded a brand new video to my Vimeo account and shared the link on social media. This new piece was still centred on glitches and 3D video game footage, but had a different tone and feel than my past creations, with more emphasis on emotional sincerity and detachment, and less on irony or sarcasm. The video's narrative also referenced the concept of the "Original Face."

I watched my post about the video accumulate Likes on Facebook. "112 Likes," I thought, reading the number in my head. "I am 112 Likes," I thought. I received more Likes, then they stopped coming in. By that point, my video was no longer new, had been pushed out of everyone's temporary attention span and into the endless scroll that was now everyday life.

38

On a cool, rainy Friday evening, I waited for my rideshare to Montreal in front of a gas station near the York Mills subway station. It was the last weekend of October. A few minutes passed, then a white van parked near the entrance. The driver, a man in his forties sporting a purple Marineland baseball cap, got out, slid the side door open and gestured for me to get in. About ten people or so were already sharing the space inside the van, all looking, I thought, miserable. After I closed the side door behind me, the man, sitting in the driver seat, covered his legs with a blanket and drove away. Exhaling, I could see my own breath, and I realized that the van's heating system wasn't functioning properly.

I tried sleeping for about an hour, but then was jolted awake by my own body, shivering. I saw that the person sitting next to me was now watching a Spider-Man movie on a tablet. To pass the time, I started watching the film on his screen, though because I didn't have access to the sound, I had to make up my own dialogue and character motivations. After maybe forty-five minutes of this, it dawned on me that maybe *Spider-Man* was secretly a story about pursuing a career as an artist. In the film, Peter Parker works a day job he dislikes so that he can afford to be Spider-Man at night, which doesn't make him money, but feels like a more meaningful use of his talents. One problem is that the more time Peter spends as Spider-Man, the more impossible it is for him to do his day job properly, because chaos from his life as Spider-Man inevitably ends up spilling into his day job.

Six hours later, I escaped the van and headed on foot towards my old apartment, which was now Val's apartment, where Grace was hanging out with her friends. Passing through the McGill campus, I couldn't help feeling happy seeing the same recognizable buildings in the same recognizable locations, like I was ingesting an antidepressant made of nostalgia. "Maybe the streets I thought I was bored of, I was actually in love with this entire time," I thought.

Arriving at my old apartment, I climbed the stairs leading to the front door and thought, "I am home," and then, "Something's wrong."

"Daniel!" said Ashlyn, emerging from the living room. "You're alive!"

"I am alive," I said.

Behind Ashlyn was Grace, who kissed me on the lips, and Roberto, who hugged me and wouldn't let go.

"Give him some air," said Ashlyn, laughing. "He just walked in."

"It's good to see you, buddy," said Roberto.

"Same," I said, smiling.

Taking off my shoes, I began noticing the changes Val had made to my apartment. I compared a mental image of my old apartment to the space I was in now, which felt like playing a game of seven errors.

"This is wild," I said. "What happened to this place?"

"I know," said Grace. "You should see the kitchen."

I peeked into the bathroom, which looked clean and insanely bright to me, probably because of the fresh layer of paint and the absence of mould on the ceiling. I went in, closed the door and peed. Flushing, I noticed that the toilet's handle had been fixed.

"It's broken," I thought. The toilet's handle was now functioning properly, and so felt broken to me.

Coming out, I glanced into the small side room, which was now Val's bedroom, and then what used to be my bedroom, which Val had transformed into a big closet.

I felt like my old apartment was in the process of forgetting me.

"It's a little disorienting being here right now," I said to Grace, sitting next to her on the couch in the living room. "I feel like everything is staring at me."

"Did you see the big closet?" said Val. "It's my favourite room now."

"I did," I said. "It's funny, I never thought of using that room as anything other than a bedroom."

"You get so much more sunlight in the little room," said Val. "Plus, I figured your old bedroom was probably the first place where you guys had sex."

"No, that was at my house," said Grace, laughing. "That's

where he told me he loved me for the first time, though. In your closet."

Val's phone rang and she moved to another room to take the call. Grace asked me if I would like to go to a show later. "I don't know if you're still doing the hiatus," she said, "but if you want to come, I am pretty sure Elliot and Jane are going to be there. They might even be playing together. Or something. The Facebook event wasn't super clear."

"I can go," I said. "I made a rule in my head that it doesn't count as partying if I am not drinking."

I wasn't sure how to explain to Grace that my sobriety was starting to feel to me less like a handicap, and more like a secret weapon.

"Okay, great," said Grace. "We're all going to dress up before leaving. Nothing too crazy since it's not Halloween yet, but they're charging less at the door if you're wearing a costume."

"What would be a basic costume that I could put together?" I said.

"I don't know," said Grace. "You're the one with the art degree. You think of something."

Joining our conversation, Ashlyn asked me if I was really coming to Newfoundland for the holidays and I said, "I am trying."

"You have to come," she said. "It's going to be so much fun. Roberto will be there too, to meet my family."

"That seems funny," I said. "Roberto in Newfoundland."

"My mom is so excited that he's coming," said Ashlyn. "She was so in love with him when she was here a few months ago."

"Maybe I should buy plane tickets to Newfoundland this weekend," I said.

"Do you think you can swing it?" said Grace.

"It's risky, but I think I can make it work," I said.

"We can look into it tomorrow," said Grace, smiling.

I got up and went to the kitchen. Pouring myself a glass of water, I noticed a big cardboard box next to the fridge. I thought about turning the box into an improvised costume, though I wasn't sure what. "Maybe a robot or something," I thought. I asked Val if she had paint. In the kitchen, I played with the box for a while, then realized I could simply paint the entire box light beige and cut holes for arms.

"I am going as a block of tofu," I told Grace 20 minutes later.

"Tofu?" said Grace.

"Yeah," I said. "It's a dumb idea, but I can't think of anything better. It'll work. It'll be funny."

A little after midnight, we left Val's apartment and walked to Psychic City, a DIY space located in a basement on St-Laurent. As we entered the venue, I recognized Jane's voice on the sound system. Wearing the box costume, I awkwardly made my way through the crowd, trying to reach the front rows. There was no stage, just a designated area where Elliot was playing slow-paced, danceable electronic music on his laptop while Jane, wearing a long white dress and a shawl, was improvising lyrics, sometimes talking, sometimes shouting things like, "Be free!" to the crowd. Behind her was a smoke machine pumping vapour into the room. From my perspective, Jane looked like an otherworldly apparition, an outline of herself, her own shadow.

39

"Playing with Elliot was such good energy," said Jane, smoking a cigarette outside the venue about two hours later. "We both loved it. Plus, I just asked that guy over there for a light in French and he totally understood me. I feel like I am on a winning streak."

Jane laughed a little.

"You should play with Elliot again," I said.

"I am pretty sure we will," said Jane. "He still has his band, so for now, this was just an experiment, but I think we're onto something."

"How have you been doing?" I said. "How are things?"

"I've been doing really good," said Jane. "I felt depressed for a while after that whole *Vice* debacle and then you leaving, but I feel re-energized now. For a while, I think I was seeing my work through the eyes of people who've made negative comments about it, so I kept censoring myself. It was like my inspiration was on death row."

"I've had that," I said.

"Other than that, I am still on social assistance, but I am not proud of it, so I want to find a way to get off," said Jane. "Lately, I've been doing this thing where I use a fake French middle name when I apply to jobs, to make sure I don't get discriminated against for being a dumb Anglo. I got a call back last week for this data entry job and the woman who left a message on my voicemail was like, 'I had a look at your résumé, maybe art isn't working out for you? Anyway, you can call me back at this number.' She made it sound like I was applying to a job that was way below me, so I felt too ashamed to return her call."

Jane laughed again. "How about you?" she said.

"I am fine," I said. "I've been going to things in Toronto, but I am still trying to get the hang of the social dynamics there. It's a little different from Montreal. I feel like more people there are afraid of being boring. It's like a whole town of people like Grace."

"When I was in Toronto last year, the people I was hanging out with kept saying 'Let's go party' and I was like, 'Okay, let's go party,'" said Jane. "But they didn't mean 'Let's go to a party.' They just meant 'Let's go to a bar.' It felt like a rip-off. That's not partying. That's just wasting money."

I laughed.

"I wanted to talk to you about that video you posted," said Jane. "I thought it was great."

"Thank you for retweeting it," I said.

"Sure thing," said Jane. "I like the part where the voiceover talks about representations of manhood and male power. It's like, you're right, the traditional male ideal is totally useless in contemporary society. We don't need buffed up warriors. We need smart, reasonable, emotionally mature human beings."

"My roommate in Toronto has all these books about Eastern philosophy for some reason, so I've been reading that a bit lately," I said. "I like the representations of masculinity in Zen Buddhism. It's like, it's okay to look at the moon and cry. It's okay to wear colourful ceremonial outfits. It's okay to explore your inner life like it's a bottomless pit."

"That's great," said Jane. "I miss going to art shows with you. It's not the same going alone, though it made me realize that I didn't want to feel jealous of anyone anymore. I was starting to fall into this trap where I would find myself hate-watching other people's work, like I would consciously look for flaws instead of opening myself up to what the other person was trying to do. Do you know what I mean?"

"That's probably 80% of the time I spend on the internet," I said.

"That jealousy, it comes from such a place of insecurity and weakness," said Jane. "Fuck that. I just don't want to feel like me and every other artist out there are fighting one another like we're in *The Hunger Games*. Someone else being successful doesn't mean that I am not. My thinking now is that I want everyone to kill it artistically, because it seems like the world would be a beautiful place if every single human was killing it artistically. Look at George W. Bush."

"You mean his paintings?" I said.

"Yeah," said Jane. "He's killing it now. Isn't it better that way?"

40

The following afternoon, I woke up in Grace's bed, with Tom-Tom sleeping between us. The cat looked still and inert like a giant plush animal, the prize of some forgotten carnival game. Grace and I had had sex the night before, though it had taken me a little longer than usual to get aroused, probably a side effect of masturbating to internet porn more frequently since moving to Toronto. "I feel like I am in a long-term relationship with internet porn and cheating on internet porn with Grace," I thought.

"So hungover," said Grace a few hours later, sitting on her bed. "Do you think you could go to the store and get me vitamin water? I would go, but it would take me at least an hour to get ready and put on makeup."

"I don't mind going to the store for you, but you shouldn't feel oppressed into having to wear makeup just to go to the corner store," I said. "The corner store guy won't care."

"I know," said Grace. "But I care."

"It's okay, I'll go," I said.

131

"Last night was fun," said Grace. "You picked a good week-end to come. Almost everyone in my friends group is coupled up now, so we don't always feel like going out. I can tell that we're all starting to slow down and party less."

"That's probably for the best," I said. "Just let it happen."

A few minutes later, I left Grace's apartment and walked to the corner store. Coming back, Grace and I discussed going to the hospital together on Monday morning to finally get her blood work done, then we looked up plane tickets to Newfoundland. I maxed out my credit card to purchase a round trip.

"Are you sure that's a good idea?" said Grace. "Are you going to be okay financially?"

"I'll figure out a way," I said. "I don't know if I like owing that much money, but I think it's worth it, so I'll manage."

"Well," said Grace. "I am happy you're coming."

Later that day, in preparation for Newfoundland, we watched the movie version of *The Shipping News*. In the film, a demure and introverted Kevin Spacey moves back to Newfoundland with his young daughter to live in an abandoned ancestral home. Grace kept talking throughout the film, trashing the movie's plot, characters and overall depiction of her homeland.

"A squid burger," she said. "I am from Newfoundland and I've never heard of a squid burger. They made that up."

CHAPTER THREE

The Shipping News

"I had to leave work a little early because I was having period cramps," read a text message from Grace. "Congratulations, you're still not a dad."

I showed up at the language school in time for my shift, but was asked by Will to come see him in his office. "It's my fault," he said. "I miscalculated." Will told me that the language school was currently losing money and that some adjustments would have to be made. Since I was still one of the most recent hires, I would have to be let go.

"Shit," I thought.

I finished my last shift, then immediately started looking for work again. I endured another round of dubious job applications and job interviews, progressively shedding my pride along the way like a snake losing its skin. About a week later, a little before mid-November, I interviewed for a job at an Indigo store in the Yorkdale Mall. Though Indigo was primarily known as a large retail bookstore, the company was in the process of diversifying its revenue. Just in time for the holidays, the store was opening a new "tech section" to sell iPads, e-readers and other things.

Though I was expecting the meeting to be short and relatively straightforward, my interviewer caught me off-guard by taking the time to go in depth. "So wait, I have to be psychoanalyzed just to get a basic job in a mall, but Rob Ford, who's the most incompetent person in the universe, is the mayor of this city?" I thought. "How does that make sense?"

Later, I received an email informing me that I would be offered a position as a "sales representative." It seemed demoralizing to be going back to an entry level, minimum wage position at this point in my life, but I needed the money enough to overcome my ego.

On the first day of training, the other new employees and I sat around a table in a conference room and watched a keynote presentation by Apple's CEO, then we had a group discussion about what we liked and didn't like about the tech giant's products. It felt like the main goal of the training program was to brainwash us all into wanting to purchase iPads. A few days later, I helped prepare the new tech section for its opening day by defeating what seemed like a sprawling empire of cardboard boxes. One box contained many pairs of gold and white headphones that looked like they belonged in some sort of high-end Swedish hotel.

That afternoon, during my lunch break, I walked around the Yorkdale Mall. I rarely went into shopping centres, so the mall felt, to me, like a kind of cultural exhibit, one whose tone was possibly cynical. "Bold, expressive and cool" read a sign in a window display at H&M. "Add a touch of glamour to your holiday wardrobe" read another. "My holiday wardrobe," I thought. "I only own one pair of pants," I thought.

"I am so happy to be sitting," I texted Grace from a bus on my way back home. "Sitting seems underrated and really cool to me right now."

The day before the new tech section's opening, Bruce, one of the store's many managers, announced that, starting tomorrow, a stricter dress code would be enforced. After work, I stopped by a thrift store and bought a light blue dress shirt and used dress shoes. Wearing my costume at work the next day, I felt like an egg, something elegant and self-contained that could shatter at any moment.

"Bold, expressive and cool," I thought.

I walked around trying to help customers and was asked by an old man, who was shaking a little, to remove a pear from his back pocket. Uninspired holiday music was playing in the entire store, and near our section was a table offering what looked like a diarrhea of copies of the same book, the autobiography of Canadian astronaut Chris Hadfield. Judging by the display, Canadian astronaut Chris Hadfield was a very powerful, very important contemporary writer who everyone should read.

Later, Bruce told me a story about Heather, Indigo's founder and public figurehead, who he had met in person a few times. "She comes in here like a smoke monster," he said. "I swear. The lights start flickering. Dogs in the parking lot start barking." Then he gave me advice on how to interact with customers, mentioning that I should never keep my arms crossed, as it didn't make me appear "likeable, open and confident."

"Well, I am not," I thought.

I accumulated shifts at the store. Describing our merchandise to consumers became a kind of routine, like the script the call centre wanted us to follow. I began smiling more, pretending I had generic opinions about our products. At work, my true self usually went into a coma, delegating my consciousness to a more pragmatic section of my brain, like the part that had learned how to tie a tie. In early December, Bruce informed me that, according to the sales report, I was "currently in the lead" and outselling all other tech employees from our store, which surprised me.

"I don't even know if that's good news or bad news," I

told Grace over text message. "The last thing I want is to be promoted."

03

An ad on Facebook kept asking me if I was "tough enough," but I never felt like I was.

04

Zen Buddhism seemed like an entire school of thought centred on the idea that "be right back" was the ultimate state of mind.

05

Examining a poster in the mall promoting the *Harry Potter* franchise, I found myself feeling increasingly sympathetic towards Voldemort, who was standing in the background and looking menacing, but also a little sad and pathetic. "He's just a weird, lonely old male bachelor who never married and doesn't have kids," I thought. "Someone get Voldemort a dog. Maybe a Pomeranian."

"The entire plot of *Harry Potter* could have been prevented by getting Voldemort a Pomeranian," I thought.

06

"Ashlyn and Roberto are getting married," Grace announced to me on Skype. It was twenty days before Christmas and fifteen days before our flight to Newfoundland. "They told everyone last night."

"For real?" I said. "Whoa, that's crazy."

"I am telling you now, but you can't talk about this," said Grace. "They don't want everyone to know, only their close friends. Everyone else will think they're still just boyfriend and girlfriend. They're only doing this now so that Roberto can stay here and be able to work legally. They're going to have a tiny courthouse wedding."

"I would do that," I said. "A tiny courthouse wedding. That seems way better to me than an actual wedding."

"Well, it's just so that they can do it quietly," said Grace. "If everything works out, they might have a real wedding in a few years. I can understand, I don't know if I would want a tiny courthouse wedding."

There was a brief pause. I thought about arguing with Grace about the merits of a "real wedding," but then decided not to.

"I am so happy for Ashlyn," said Grace. "I was probably way too excited when she told us last night, but we've always had a sister-like relationship, so I felt like it was a big moment. I felt like it was okay for me to jump and be happy."

"Wait, if you have a sister-like relationship with Ashlyn, does that mean Roberto is going to be my brother-like-in-law?" I said.

"It can," said Grace.

07

Over email, I told Bruce that I would be flying to Newfoundland for the holidays and would be unavailable for a period of ten days. In a lengthy response message, Bruce explained that, as a company rule, Indigo didn't allow time off for anyone during the holidays, meaning that he would be unable to accommodate my request.

"No one told me, so I had no idea," I wrote back, "but that makes sense. If there's really no other way to resolve this, I'll just resign."

Later, I informed Jane via text message that I had just quit my dumb job. "That's awesome news, I am happy for you," she replied, which seemed like a good example of our priorities.

08

Convincing myself I was a "good artist" while also knowing how pointless it was to be one.

09

Alternate universe in which the 1995 movie *Waterworld* wasn't a box office flop, causing instant, worldwide acceptance of its important message about the dangers of global warming.

10

Facebook should be re-classified as a public park.

11

Barely awake and sitting on a bench at the airport, I felt like I was functioning using only my spatial memory, like a bee. On the wall in front of me was a riddle-like advertisement for Louis Vuitton that featured a wealthy white man smiling smugly in front of two models wearing gold masks. "Luxury clothing," I thought. "I only own one pair of pants," I thought. It was 7 a.m. and I had travelled in a Megabus overnight, slept for about an hour at Grace's apartment and then cabbed with her to the airport. I hadn't been up at this hour in a long time, felt like this 7 a.m. didn't "seem right," as if it was a hoax, something that had been staged, like a fake moon landing.

Turning around, I saw that Grace, who had gone to the bathroom, was now chatting with a random airport employee. The employee made a joke and Grace laughed. Watching her interact with the man, I felt like she was socializing at an elite level, the equivalent, maybe, of a basketball player reaching the NBA.

"Talking is her art form," I thought.

"Want one?" said Grace a few minutes later, retrieving a clementine from her bag.

"I am okay," I said.

"The first time I flew on a plane," said Grace, "I remember, I was eight. I couldn't believe that we were above the clouds instead of under them. It seemed so reckless to me, like we were messing with the natural order of things."

I liked Grace's anecdote, but felt too tired to laugh. Grace seemed to be in a good mood and full of energy. Maybe, I thought, it was because her life over the past year or so had gained the kind of coherent, movie-like narrative that real life rarely has, though always seems to be yearning to have. This year, she was going home for the holidays not by herself, always a counter-argument for the voice in her head trying to convince her that she was finally getting her shit together, but with her boyfriend, who she had been dating for almost a year, and who she thought her family would approve of. As a subplot in her life, one of her best friends was getting married for the sole purpose of getting citizenship, which still seemed powerful and romantic. She was also expecting her younger sister and her boyfriend to finally announce their engagement during the holidays.

"They've been together since high school," said Grace, handling most of the conversation. "He told her he wouldn't propose to her on a holiday, but maybe that's just to throw her off. I feel like so much is going on right now. Roberto and Ashlyn. My sister and her boyfriend. It's strange to see everyone I grew up with getting into all these serious life situations."

"I know what you mean," I said. "Maybe we should get a mortgage together, just to keep up with people."

"If you want," said Grace, smiling.

"Do you think your friends are all subtly competing with one another?" I said. "Like, who can be the most adult the fastest?"

"I don't know, I don't think so," said Grace. "Although I guess I am sort of upset that my little sister is going to have a kid way before me. She's on the fast track to extreme motherhood."

"What does your dad think of your sister's boyfriend?" I said.

"Oh, he loves him," said Grace. "Colin is awesome. I should warn you about one thing, though. At my dad's house, it's possible that we won't be allowed to sleep in the same room because we're not married. It's this dumb rule he has. I hope that's okay with you."

"That's fine, I guess," I said. "In general, I think I want to go with whatever makes your dad least angry."

"Thank you," said Grace. "Dad has this whole thing. Even my sister and her boyfriend, they live together and they're practically married and they still have to sleep in separate rooms when they stay at my dad's house."

"It shouldn't be too bad," I said. "We'll manage. God, I can't wait to fall asleep in the plane. We should infiltrate that line of people over there. They're boarding right now."

"That's Turkish Airlines," said Grace.

"Turkish Airlines sounds good," I said. "Maybe they could drop us off in California or something."

"Where we're going is pretty much the opposite of California," said Grace.

12

"That's how we know we're in Newfoundland," said Grace, pointing out an ad in the airport for Mary Brown's, a chain of local restaurants that looked to me like some sort of feminist KFC.

"It's so nice to finally meet you," said Lindsay, Grace's sister, about ten minutes later. She had black hair, was wearing a brown hooded jacket with a fur trim and physically resembled her sister, though was proportionally smaller, like a Russian doll of Grace.

"How was the flight?" Lindsay asked.

"It was fine for the most part," said Grace. "Daniel had a little incident."

"Everything okay?" said Lindsay.

"Yeah, yeah," said Grace. "It was nothing. We were about to land and he was trying to sleep, and then all of sudden I see him crouching down and holding his eye in pain. I was like, 'What's wrong?'"

"You were petting my back a little," I said, laughing.

"I didn't know what to do," said Grace. "I thought something had gone into your eye."

"It was just the pressure change," I said. "It's weird, I've never had problems flying before. I almost wanted to ask you to do the Heimlich manoeuvre on my eye."

"But you're okay now?" asked Lindsay.

"I am fine," I said.

"Good," said Lindsay. "Do you need to get your suitcase?"

"Oh, all I brought is this backpack," I said. "I like to travel light."

"Daniel lives frugally in general," Grace explained. "He's the kind the person who would live the same way whether he makes $8,000 or $800,000 per year."

"Well, okay then," said Lindsay. "Come!"

We followed Lindsay and exited the airport. Outside, it was cold and snowy, with wind coming at us from every direction. "Welcome to Newfoundland," said Lindsay, her tone implying a kind of sarcastic resignation.

"Oh my god, it's freezing outside," said Grace once inside Lindsay's car.

"The car is going to warm up soon," Lindsay replied. She didn't have a strong regional accent, except for when using words like "car," which she pronounced "câar."

"The heat's on maximum," Lindsay added. "It's always on maximum."

Leaving the parking lot, Grace and her sister began chatting in a seemingly nonstop manner. From the backseat, I listened to a song by the band Majical Cloudz, which was playing through an iPhone plugged into the car stereo, and contemplated my surroundings. I was so used to tall buildings obstructing my view that the sky in Newfoundland seemed dangerously low to me, like it was about to fall off itself.

On our way to Mount Pearl, where Grace's dad's house was located, we passed Cape Spear, which, Grace specified in a brief aside, was the "easternmost point in Canada." Later, I noticed on the side of the road a store that appeared to be selling fireworks and ice cream, then another whose message board was simply advertising "Milk," as every other letter had been blown away by the wind. I was shocked by how clearly I could see trees in the distance, felt like they were coming directly at me, like I was wearing 3D glasses. In the city, nature often seemed, to me, like an imaginary concept within a default reality of human beings, technology and buildings. Here, it seemed, maybe nature was the default reality, and human beings were the imaginary concept.

13

"Ye can take your things to the bedrooms downstairs," said Grace's dad's girlfriend, who was named Martha. She had long hair, was maybe in her mid-fifties, and spoke with a heavy regional accent, often mashing her words together like a kind of baby food.

"Wait," said a stupefied Grace. "'Ye' means the both of us."

Before Martha could clarify whether or not we would be allowed to share a bedroom, Grace grabbed her suitcase and gestured for me to follow her lead. The downstairs bedroom was furnished with a bed, a bedside table, a dresser and an exercise machine. Grace's dad's house, which he had purchased only the year before, contained, among other rooms, a large kitchen connected to a living room, spare bedrooms, a recreational area and a bar. Compared to my tiny apartment in Toronto, the space felt, to me, infinite.

"She was definitely telling us that we can both take our things downstairs," said Grace. "Well, I think. I hope I am right."

"Just ask your dad," I said.

"I kind of don't want to," said Grace. "He can't take it back if I don't ask him."

"Is this you?" I said, picking up a framed photo of a younger Grace with wavy hair and braces.

"This is so embarrassing," said Grace. "I completely forgot about this. Feel free to pretend you didn't see this."

"What are you talking about, this is great," I said. "I feel like that's exactly why we came here. To look at embarrassing photos of you."

"Well," said Grace. "You're in for a treat, if that's the case."

"What's happening in this one?" I said, picking up another photo.

"This is me and my grade 4 boyfriend," said Grace. "I say boyfriend, but that's probably not the right word. All it was is that we would see each other once every two weeks at these dances. We would slow-dance together."

"It sounds better than most relationships I've had," I said.

"Yeah," said Grace. "Me too, now that I think about it."

About twenty minutes passed. Back upstairs, we sat in the living room with Lindsay, Martha and Grace's dad, who was named Walter and had thick eyebrows. He was wearing a black sweater with the logo of a beer company on it. "So I says to her, I clicks on it and then I reads it," Martha said, telling a story that involved a computer file. She sometimes inserted the letter s after certain words like she was trying it out, wanted to see if she liked it.

Walter offered me a beer, which I politely declined without mentioning the hiatus. This seemed to confuse him, as if he hadn't considered the possibility of me saying no. Looking at the television screen, I noticed that a Christmas movie starring Ben Affleck was currently playing.

"I am not sure why anyone would want to watch Ben Affleck be happy for Christmas," I said.

"Yeah, that movie is some' stupid," said Martha. "So, my boy, it's your first time in Newfoundland, what do you think so far?"

"It's nice," I said. "When we were outside earlier, I took a deep breath and actual oxygen came into my lungs instead of pollution. It felt good."

"You grew up in Montreal, you probably speak French," said Martha. "You should teach Grace some French."

"I speak French enough to get by, but that's it," I said.

"What do your parents think about you coming all the way here to Newfoundland?" said Martha.

"Oh, I am not close to my family anymore," I said. "I actually haven't had a traditional Christmas in a few years. Last year, I did, like, nothing."

"Well," said Martha, looking disappointed. "You're welcome here."

Out of nowhere, Walter got up quickly, retrieved a broom from a closet and began sweeping the floor. "Lindsay, can I talk to you?" said Grace before moving to another room with her sister. For a little while, I watched television alone with Martha and found myself mesmerized by the commercials. I hadn't watched television on a television in a long time, so the alternate reality depicted by the commercials, in which artificial human beings had extraordinary reactions to consumer products, seemed eccentric and fascinating to me. "Were TV commercials always like that?" I thought. "Maybe they were always like that," I thought.

About an hour later, we sat around the kitchen table and ate lobster and various salads. Walter told a story, gleefully, it seemed, about Grace devouring an entire lemon meringue pie as a teenager, then hiding the empty dish in her room. Grace defensively fact-checked the anecdote in real time, specifying that it was "half a pie" and "in several sittings."

After dinner, Lindsay's boyfriend and Grace's grandparents, who lived in a house across the street, joined us. Walter opened his liquor cabinet, offering drinks to everyone. I sat on the couch in the living room, bracketed between Grace and her grandparents. I sensed that Grace's family was observing how Grace and I were interacting as a couple, making me feel like we were performing "being a couple" in front of them, as if our visit to Newfoundland also doubled as an advertisement for our relationship.

A different Christmas movie, this one starring Will Ferrell, was now playing on television. Looking at me, Grace's grandma said, "Let me tell you some', my boy," then whispered in my ear that I was a "very handsome man." She laughed out loud to herself, then Grace laughed, then I tried to laugh, then Will Ferrell on television laughed.

Later, I tried to chat with Grace's grandfather, who was wearing a cool hat that said "I'd rather be fishing" along with an illustration of a bass jumping, something I probably would have bought if I had found it in a bin at a thrift store. Because of his heavy regional accent, Grace's grandfather and I had difficulty communicating. His mouth barely moved when speaking, making his sentences sound to me something like, "Na na na go vadada, na na na na, Whitney's daughter."

On a few occasions, I had no idea what to respond and found myself borrowing Roberto's strategy, simply saying "wow" while nodding.

"My Nan loves you," said Grace. "It's cute."

"I like how your dad seems determined to get me wasted," I said. "He keeps offering me beer. I feel like he's threatening me with beer."

"He's just being polite," said Grace. "I am amazed that he hasn't put up the photo of me and my Australian boyfriend somewhere. He loves that photo. When I was still living with him, I remember, whenever I would take it down, he would just put it back up later. We would have Kevin over for dinner and the first thing he would see is this big photo of Martin and me looking happy forever."

"Is she telling you about Martin?" said Grace's dad, popping into the conversation.

"No," said Grace. "No, I wasn't."

"Oh," said Walter. "Well, Martin was a nice boy."

"I invited some friends from high school to come over later," said Grace. "I might have to leave you on your own for a while, but let me know if my family is being insane to you. I'll talk to them."

"I'll be alright," I said.

Grace got up and walked to her dad's alcohol cabinet. Trying to make herself a mojito, she began fighting a little with her dad, who wanted to give her advice on how to make the drink. "Dad, I am okay," said Grace, sounding annoyed. "I work in a pub, I know what I am doing with alcohol."

"Just tryin' to be helpful, dear," said Walter. "I don't know why you'all getting upset."

More guests arrived, including various relatives, family friends and Ashlyn's mom, Diane, who I had met a few months earlier. I went to the bathroom. When I returned, I saw that, aside from Grace's grandparents, who were sitting together on the living room couch, both grinning, it seemed, at the room around them, the men were now huddled around Walter's alcohol cabinet while the women were forming a separate group on the other side of the room. Different generations were interacting with one another, with the men looking alike, the women also looking alike.

I felt pressured to join the men's group, though I wasn't sure we would have much in common.

Grace's cousin, Luke, who was sporting a UFC t-shirt featuring airbrushed men trapped inside a cage, was telling a story about ski-dooing somewhere, then ski-dooing back. Colin, Lindsay's boyfriend, said, "That's deadly," aloud and the men laughed.

I laughed a little, then pictured myself hopping onto a ski-doo and speeding away from this conversation.

"Do you like football, Daniel?" Colin asked me, trying to include me in the conversation.

"I am not much of a sports fan," I said.

"Why not?" said Luke.

"I don't know," I said. "I always feel like sports fans are faking it. It doesn't really matter who wins or loses, it's more about sharing a moment with other people. Not feeling alone."

"You see," said Colin, "I didn't get football before either, but then I started watching it a few years ago and it's so great."

"I just love Sundays when they have twelve hours of football on," said Luke.

"So yeah, give football a shot," said Colin.

"I will," I said.

In the living room, Diane, who looked inebriated and seemed to be enjoying herself, decided to put on the song "Blurred Lines." She began dancing by herself in the middle of the room, then was joined by Grace's dad, who was laughing.

Eventually, Diane got Grace's grandfather to get up from the couch and dance with her. His attempt at dancing looked like a combination of "bewildered" and "in pain."

Leaving the men's group, I sat next to Grace, who introduced me to a friend of hers from high school. Looking at her phone, Lindsay mentioned that she had recorded a video of Diane dancing and sent it through Snapchat to Ashlyn, adding the caption, "This is your mom partying."

"Oh yeah, I asked Lindsay about the room," said Grace. "Apparently, Dad ended up changing his mind at the last minute, so we're allowed to sleep in the same bed. He told Lindsay that maybe it was time 'to let go of that foolishness.'"

"That seems bold of your dad," I said, which made me think of Walter as "bold, expressive and cool."

"It was mostly a rule that Dad was enforcing because of Nan's religious values," said Grace. "He didn't want his mom to disapprove."

"Does your grandma hate me for not believing in anything?" I said.

"She loves you right now," said Grace. "Just don't talk to her about religion. Don't tell her you think the Satanic Temple makes sense. Pretend you're a good Christian boy if she asks."

"Sure," I said. "The Lord is my whatever."

14

Around 3 a.m., I helped Grace, who was drunk, travel safely down the stairs and reach the bed in our room. Crash-landing on the mattress, we automatically began kissing and removing items of clothing. "Are we sure we're doing this?" I said, laughing. "Your dad didn't want us to sleep in the same room exactly for that reason."

"Take your pants the fuck off," said Grace.

We had sex, which seemed more unpredictable than usual, the same two bodies multiplying but producing, somehow, a different result. Grace and I had orgasms at almost the same time, and though I was able to pull out in time, I came close to ejaculating inside her.

"Shit," I thought, lying next to Grace in the dark about thirty minutes later. "I don't think I actually came inside her, but it was probably close." Just to be safe, I tried to calculate in my head whether or not it would even be physically possible for her to become pregnant right now. I couldn't remember the exact date of her last period and didn't have the password to her phone to check the period app.

15

Afraid.

16

While Grace was in the shower, I sat in the kitchen with my laptop. "Have you got yourself a good night sleep?" Martha asked me. It was the following afternoon and Grace and I were about to head over to her grandma's house, who had invited us for toutons, a treat made of fried bread dough. In the living room, Walter was watching local news on television. The lonely news anchor was reporting an outbreak of "salmon anemia." Glancing at my computer screen, Martha asked what I was working on. I wasn't sure how to explain my art practice to her, so as a joke, I said I was finishing *The Shipping News 2*, a video art sequel to the movie *The Shipping News*, but Martha took me at face value and said, "Sounds nice." She mentioned being impressed that I was working despite being "on vacation," which made me realize that I had completely failed to think of Newfoundland as a "vacation" until now. I explained that I enjoyed working on things, was pretty much always "working on things," and so that it rarely felt like work to me.

"That's good, Walter," said Martha to her partner. "He ain't lazy."

About an hour passed. Putting on her winter jacket, Grace mentioned that just the thought of having to step outside was making her feel "pre-cold." As we crossed the snow-covered street to reach her grandparents' house, which was yellow, I told Grace that I wasn't entirely sure I had pulled out in time the night before and asked if she could take Plan в. "I can pay for it," I said. "It's my fault."

"I can take it," said Grace, "but it fucks up my period and it makes me feel like shit. It's really not the best."

"I am, like, 90% sure I pulled out in time," I said, "but I think I'd feel better if you took it, if that's okay."

"I was so drunk," said Grace. "I don't remember anything."

Later, we sat around a wooden table in her grandparents' kitchen. While Grace was chatting with her grandma, I contemplated the room around me, which was decorated with pictures of babies looking scared, a cross, a painting of *The Last Supper,* plastic figurines of Santa Claus and Jesus sitting together in a swing set, a faded picture of a man standing next to a horse and a framed inspirational image that said "A smile is beautiful, doesn't cost a cent."

"What are you looking at?" said Grace in a playful tone, addressing me. "You probably think it's so funny that Nan doesn't have a computer or Wi-Fi."

"I wouldn't know what to do with it!" said Grace's grandma, laughing.

"Daniel pretty much lives inside his computer," said Grace.

"Oh, does he now?" said Grace's grandma.

"It's true," I said. "Sometimes it's almost like I am surprised that I exist."

In the nearby living room, Grace's grandfather was watching *The Price is Right*. On television, an attractive woman wearing a cocktail dress was presenting an electric blender as if the blender was a famous and affluent celebrity.

I imagined the blender having its own Christmas movie, like Ben Affleck.

"*The Smoothie on 34th Street*," I thought as a potential title for the film.

"Did I tell you that Dad really wanted to screech you in last night?" Grace said. "He loves to do the ceremony to screech people in. It's like theatre for him. I told him that we want to screech Roberto and you at the same time, but last night, he wouldn't hear it. He was like, 'I am getting my paddle and screeching Daniel in right now.' I had to talk him out of it."

"Oh, right," I said. "I forgot that I have to get screeched in."

"Yeah, you're pretty much going to have to put up with it," she said. "Sorry. It won't be that bad. Well, maybe it'll be a little bad, but at least Roberto will do it with you, so it'll be funny."

About thirty minutes later, we helped Grace's grandma set up the table for lunch. Before eating, we collectively thanked an imaginary being for our meal, which made me picture myself following the same ritual at home, saying grace before eating rushed food in front of my laptop alone. After we finished eating, we moved to the living room, where Grace examined her grandfather's old acoustic guitar, letting her fingers feel the strings.

"You should play something," I said. "I've never even heard you play guitar."

"I don't know what to play," said Grace. "I was never any good at improvising on the fly. I would always draw a blank."

"Just play something simple," I said. "Play a Christmas song. Play 'Sweet Caroline.'"

"'Sweet Caroline' is not a Christmas song," said Grace.

"I just meant, play anything," I said.

"Okay, I'll try," said Grace.

She began playing an acoustic version of "Deck the Halls" with surprising poise and confidence, a side of her I wasn't used to seeing. A few minutes later, she transitioned into "Jingle Bells" and I went back to the kitchen to help Grace's grandma clean dishes. "Grace is such a good girl," her grandma said to me. "She hasn't been lucky, but she has a great heart."

She praised Grace at length to me, in a tone I kept interpreting as, "Please marry our granddaughter, someone really should."

17

Waiting in line at the pharmacy, I glanced at magazine covers with faces of celebrities on them and wondered if celebrities were just a type of visual pollution. Via text message, I told Jane about Grace taking Plan B. Jane replied, "So she's not going to carry your unborn spawn to term?" and I texted back a bomb emoji and then a baby emoji.

18

"Sorry I am such a bad driver, guys," said Lindsay, who was driving cautiously. It was the following night and we were on our way to Diane's house to visit Ashlyn and Roberto, who had arrived in Newfoundland that day.

"You're doing fine," I said. "You're a great driver. You could be a character in *Mario Kart*."

"He's right," said Colin. "You're too tense when you're driving."

"Lindsay is always afraid of everything," said Grace. "She even has this irrational fear of planes. She doesn't like it when she's driving and there's a plane flying over her head. She'll just pull up on the side of the road and wait until the plane's gone."

"Shut up, you don't get it," said Lindsay. "They're dangerous."

"Oh, I haven't listened to this song in so long," said Colin, turning up the volume on the car stereo. "Wake Up" by Arcade Fire began playing loudly in the car. "That song's deadly."

Colin grew excited, started bouncing up and down in his seat. From the backseat, I pushed him a little, like we were in a mosh pit at a concert, and he pushed me back. I pushed Grace playfully, who pushed Colin, who pushed me again. Everyone in the car except Lindsay, who desperately wanted to avoid crashing her car into a plane, was laughing and moshing to the rhythm of the song.

Arriving at Diane's house in St. John's, Lindsay parked her car on the side of the road. Getting out, I heard a body of water rustling in the distance, then a cold, miserable wind blew through me. I thought about how there was something sooth-ing about the combinations of these sounds, like I was hearing the universe inhaling and exhaling.

"I can't believe you're not freezing," said Grace, commen-ing on my outfit. I was wearing regular shoes, didn't own win-ter boots or mittens.

"I am a little cold, but it's not like we're going on an expedi-tion or something," I said. "I'll be fine."

"Your feet must be so wet," said Grace. "I don't know how you do it."

"My trick is, I don't have a body," I said.

"Come on in, guys," said Ashlyn, greeting us at the door. Entering the house and removing my jacket, I spotted Roberto in the kitchen, chatting with a man in his fifties, probably Ashlyn's father. "Default guy friend," I thought. Ashlyn gave us a quick tour of her mom's house, which was spacious and decorated with an attention to detail that was not unlike, I thought, the way I crafted my social media presence online. Around the house, family members and friends of different age groups were socializing and drinking. Ashlyn, Grace, Colin, Lindsay and I sat in the living room. Around us were two leather couches, a colourful rug, a framed newspaper clipping of a teenage Ashlyn smiling after winning a local fashion design competition, a painting of a boat and a Christmas tree that looked supersized, as if it had been genetically modified.

"Memory," I thought, examining the boat painting.

"That's what I love about this place," said Ashlyn. "There's so much space. It's so easy to break away from the parents. They can do their thing over there and we can do our thing over here."

Listening to Ashlyn talk, I thought about how she still viewed the generation above her as "the parents" and her circle of friends as "the children," how it was probably one of the last few years she would be able to make this distinction.

Ashlyn's father, who was named Phil, approached our group and asked me if I wanted anything to drink. I declined his offer and he reacted in a similar manner to Grace's dad, his expression a combination of disappointment and incomprehension.

"I feel like I am blowing everyone's mind when they offer me a beer and I turn it down," I said to Grace.

"Are you sure you don't want anything?" said Grace. "Diane and Phil are loaded, so don't feel bad about asking. You can have anything you want. Drinks, food, anything. Just ask."

"Maybe that's part of the problem," I said. "I am so used to buying whatever's the cheapest option that it's like I don't even know how to want anymore. It's almost overwhelming when there's more than one option now."

"Phil is just trying to be a good host," said Grace.

"I know," I said, "and I appreciate how generous everyone is, I am just disoriented. It's like I went from poverty line to middle class overnight."

About an hour passed. Chatting with Grace, Ashlyn mentioned a murder mystery dinner that her mom was organizing. "Mom loves murder mysteries," she said. "She wants to have one while Roberto is here. It's a little kitschy, but it could be fun. I don't know. Would you and Daniel want to do it?"

"Yeah, probably," said Grace.

Ashlyn's cousin, Ben, and his wife, Emily, joined our group. They were about the same age as Grace and I, were married and had two daughters, ages 2 and 6. I interacted with Ben's oldest daughter for a little while, and it dawned on me that in Newfoundland, I felt like I was part of a natural hierarchy. This was different from my everyday life, where I felt mostly ageless and disconnected from traditional age markers, like a branch that had been ripped from its generational tree. In my normal life, I rarely felt any pressure to get married, but here, in Newfoundland, it suddenly seemed as if getting married to Grace right now could make perfect sense.

"It's funny to see you playing with a kid," said Grace. "You're good at it."

"I have no idea what I am doing," I said.

"Daniel," said Phil, placing a hand on my shoulder. "It's Daniel, right? We need you for something."

"You need me?" I said.

"Yes, I need you and I need Ben," said Phil. "You two. It's very important. Just follow me."

"Alright," I said. I got up and followed Phil down a hall and into what seemed to be an activities room. Roberto was standing next to a game board in the shape of an octagon.

"Okay, boys," said Phil. "We're playing crokinole. It's a board game that's a little bit like curling."

"It's great," said Ben. "You'll love it. We can do Team Mexico vs. Team Newfoundland."

Phil immediately began explaining the rules. In a game of crokinole, I was told, players took turns firing discs with their fingers, trying to get the discs to land in the higher-scoring regions of the board.

"That's it, it's that simple," said Phil. "If you don't under-stand how to play this, you're dumber than a box of donuts."

"Wow," said Roberto.

"Here we go," said Phil.

It was determined that Team Mexico, which was composed of Roberto and I, would go first. Using my index finger, I launched a disc across the game board and then waited for Phil's reaction, which would tell me whether I was playing poorly or very well. "Oh, looks like we got ourselves a pro over here," said Phil, making me feel like I was excelling at this game. "Team Captain," I thought, imagining Roberto and me representing Mexico together at some sort of World Cup.

Phil played next, followed by Roberto, then Ben, then me again. Before his second attempt, Roberto studied the board carefully, trying to play in a more strategic manner. Phil, showing impatience, said, "Roberto, let's go!" and then clapped his hands twice and added, "Arriba! Arriba!" Trying to be funny, Phil sometimes addressed Roberto using stereotypical Spanish-sounding words, which seemed unnecessary and mildly offensive.

After the game, which Team Mexico lost in a swift and decisive manner to Team Newfoundland, I heard noise coming from the living room, including laughter. Returning from the games room, I saw Grace's dad in the entrance wearing a fisherman outfit, complete with rubber boots, a yellow hat and a wooden paddle.

"Here they are," Walter shouted, pointing at Roberto and me.

"Roberto, Daniel, come on!" said Ashlyn, laughing. "You guys are getting screeched in!"

Roberto and I exchanged brief, uncomfortable grins. Everyone gathered in the living room. "I am so filming this," said Grace, retrieving her phone from her handbag. I wasn't sure I wanted videos of the ceremony to appear online, didn't know how they would mesh with my usual social media presence. Trying to get the small crowd to quiet down, Walter shouted, "Okay, okay, okay," while stomping the ground with his right foot. Next to him, Roberto and I were standing in silence, awaiting what seemed to us like both a punishment and a reward. Walter welcomed everyone to tonight's "special event," then invited Roberto and I to put on yellow overalls. Once in costume, we were told to get on our knees and then asked to confirm that we wanted to become honorary New-foundlanders. The correct answer to this question, and to most of the following questions, Walter informed us, was "yes, b'y."

"So here we have little Quebec boy, is that right?" Walter said, placing his hand on my head.

"Yes, b'y," I said, sounding defeated.

"Oh, that Newfie accent's gonna need some practice," said Walter. "And this is little Mexican boy, yeah?"

"Yes," said Roberto, with a look of terrified determination on his face. "No. I mean, yes, b'y."

"That Newfie accent's gonna need lots of practice, my boy," said Walter, making the crowd laugh. Addressing the room, Walter began telling everyone "a story about a Newfie," which was more or less an unrelated dirty joke involving someone's sister being sexually promiscuous. Next, Walter gave Roberto and I a small piece of hard bread to eat, then asked us if we wanted our "Newfie steak," which was a slice of baloney, "thick" or "thin."

"Daniel, thick or thin?" said Walter.

"Thin," I said.

"Thin!" repeated Walter, handing me a slice. "Roberto, thick or thin?"

"Think," said Roberto, nervously mixing up the two answers, which drew laughter. "Thick."

"Thick it is!" said Walter.

For his next trick, Grace's dad retrieved a frozen cod from a cooler and explained that we would have to kiss the fish on its lips. Someone in the crowd gasped while the rest of the room cheered and applauded. Walter held the fish close to my face and I gave it a quick kiss without hesitating, thinking we would reach the end of the ceremony faster.

Many pictures were taken of me kissing the fish.

Roberto did the same, then Walter handed us shots of Screech, a type of rum sold in Newfoundland. Before ingesting the drink, he asked us to repeat a long sentence of impenetrable Newfoundland jargon that ended with the words "big jib draw." Roberto and I struggled to replicate the chain of sounds, then emptied our shot glasses.

As the liquor slid down my throat, I realized that this was the first time I had drunk alcohol in months and that I had technically just ended my party hiatus.

"Welcome to Newfoundland!" Ashlyn shouted, with the rest of the crowd cheering.

"Welcome to Newfoundland!" someone else shouted.

"Welcome to Newfoundland, Daniel," said Walter, turning to me and smiling. "It'd be nice to have a little Quebec boy in the family."

19

"I don't know what this province is doing to me," said Grace after another copious dinner at her dad's house. Martha had made fish and brewis for everyone using the cod I had kissed the night before. "I am going to put on a thousand pounds while we're here."

"It makes sense that you want to eat more than usual," I said. "It's free food and there's so much of it."

"As soon as we get back, I am doing salads and yoga," said Grace. "No way I am getting fat again. Would you even like me if I was big?"

"I don't know," I said.

"Hey," said Grace. "That's not nice."

"No, I just mean, I have no way of knowing," I said. "I don't know if I would like you if you were anorexic either."

Grace didn't seem happy with my answer. Two hours passed. Grace had heartburn and made ginger tea to help her stomach settle. We borrowed DVDs from her dad, but then couldn't agree on which film to watch. Grace was okay with watching any of them while I felt lukewarm about all of them.

"Come on, pick something," said Grace.

"All the movies look stupid," I said.

"Well, let's watch something stupid," said Grace. "Who cares?"

"Alright, fuck it," I said. "Whatever."

We tried the movie *This is 40*, which Lindsay had recommended to Grace. In the film, a middle-aged married couple stuck in an adversarial relationship struggle with money, worry about their two daughters and generally seem to tolerate their lives more than enjoy them.

"This is fucking terrible," I said about halfway through the movie.

"What are you talking about?" said Grace. "It's a little cliché, but I don't think it's bad. The dialogue is funny."

"It just feels so lazy," I said. "It's like a movie producer somewhere went, 'How do most people imagine life at forty?' and then just put that onscreen. And now people watch this and it reinforces their idea of what a person's life at forty should be like, so more movie producers out there will think, 'How do most people imagine life at forty?' and create other movies exactly like this one. It's like an infinite loop."

"Well, what would you have done?" said Grace.

"I don't know," I said. "I feel like a movie called *This Isn't 40* would have been better. Television and movies always try to show you what your life should be like at different stages, but you're probably better off ignoring them entirely, because then you'll have no definition of what your life should or shouldn't be. Your life can be whatever. You can be forty-two and decide to live in a squat with punk roommates or randomly move to Japan. It's all okay. Your life is always okay."

"So you would have made a movie about Paul Rudd moving to Japan?" said Grace.

"No," I said. "I mean, yeah, maybe."

On Christmas morning, I was surprised to discover that Martha had prepared a stocking for me, which she had hung next to Grace's. The stocking contained a toothbrush, an orange, some assorted chocolates and two pairs of socks.

"This is just a little some'," said Martha of the stocking. "Your real gift is under the tree."

"I get a real gift?" I said.

"Yes, b'y," said Martha, looking proud of herself.

"This is too much," I said. "I was honestly happy with just the toothbrush."

Martha laughed, but I wasn't joking.

"My life right now feels like an insane Ben Affleck Christmas movie in which I come to Newfoundland to learn the true meaning of Christmas," I said to Grace.

Later, Grace's grandparents joined us and we started unwrapping presents. Martha and Walter received a box of alcoholic chocolates from me, Lindsay got futuristic-looking dinnerware from her dad and I received what seemed to be an impromptu gift from Grace's grandparents, a $20 bill tucked inside a greeting card. When I opened the present, Grace's grandma winked at me, making me feel like the money was a kind of bribe.

Part of my gift for Grace was a large illustration that I had spent a lot of time making and then printed on high-quality paper and framed. The illustration was titled "The nine lives of Tom-Tom" and detailed with text and drawings the multiple personalities of her cat. One personality was "undercover cop Tom-Tom," with Tom-Tom monitoring us sleeping in her bed, while another was "blockbuster Tom-Tom," with Tom-Tom looking amused and entertained by the nothing happening outside of Grace's bedroom window.

"This is the best thing I've ever seen," said Grace, inspecting the illustration. "Very accurate depiction of my cat."

"I didn't have a lot of money to work with, so I thought I could add a homemade thing to my gift," I said.

"I didn't even care if you got me anything," said Grace. "Your gift to me could have been you buying a plane ticket to be here with me and that would have been fine. That would have been perfect."

21

On Boxing Day, Andrea, Grace, Ashlyn, Roberto and I shared a cab from Lindsay's apartment to The Ship, a pub in St. John's. Though it wasn't very late, the main room in the bar was already almost at full capacity. Onstage, a music group made up of heavy-set men in their forties were playing an unspectacular but serviceable cover of "Have You Ever Seen the Rain?" to the delight of the crowd. Since the hiatus was over, I allowed myself to order a pint of beer, which I drank more slowly than usual. When the song ended, the singer asked the crowd if anyone had any requests and I yelled "Radiohead" and then "Björk," making myself laugh by imagining the men spontaneously deciding to cover all of *Medúlla*.

Around 1 a.m., I returned from the bathroom and scanned the main room looking for Grace, but could only spot Roberto, who seemed, for some reason, to be having an argument with a bartender. Roberto was laughing while being yelled at, trying to use laughter to defuse the tension. I headed in Roberto's direction to see what the problem was, but the conversation ended before I could reach the bar. Seeing me approaching, Roberto immediately asked if I would like to go outside with him.

"What happened in there?" I said a few minutes later. Snow-flakes of various shapes and sizes were falling on us, and there was little to no wind.

"That guy," said Roberto, "he's an old boyfriend of Ashlyn. He was jealous. I wanted to order a beer, but he said he didn't understand my accent and I should get out of his bar. Yo, it was crazy."

"Has anyone else been an asshole to you since you got here?" I said.

"No, everyone has been so nice," said Roberto. "Some people don't understand my accent and I have to say, 'I am from Mexico.' Then they ask me questions about Mexico."

"I am sure they're fascinated by you," I said.

"Some people, they look at me like I am from the moon," said Roberto, laughing.

"I wasn't sure if Ashlyn's dad was making you feel uncomfortable," I said. "He kept saying Spanish things to you that sounded like a Speedy Gonzales cartoon."

"No," said Roberto. "Phil was just trying to be funny. Also, I love Speedy."

"You do?" I said.

"Yeah," said Roberto. "Speedy is Mexican. He's smart. He runs fast."

"I guess that makes sense," I said. "I always thought Speedy was a bad caricature of a Mexican person, but there are probably not that many Mexican cartoon characters. Iron Man isn't Mexican. The Lion King isn't Mexican. Might as well embrace this one."

"Can I tell you something about Newfoundland?" said Roberto, crushing a snowflake with his left hand. "I love the snow. Snow was like a myth for me growing up. My parents,

166

if the weather was minus something, they would be talking about it for a week."

I asked Roberto what his parents thought of his wedding and he said that they were happy for him and that they had purchased plane tickets to come visit him in Montreal in February, which was when Ashlyn and he would officially be getting married. Roberto said that his mom had never left Mexico, but that his Dad had visited Canada once, travelling to Ottawa as part of a business delegation.

We continued chatting outside for a while, then were interrupted by Andrea, Grace and Ashlyn, who had been looking for us.

"What are you guys doing out here?" said Grace.

"We're just talking," I said. "Do you want to go?"

"You want to leave?" said Grace.

"Yeah, it's busy and awful in there," I said.

"Well, I know it's not cool Montreal bands playing, but keep an open mind," said Grace.

"No, it's not that," I said. "I am fine with the music. It's just, I don't know if I want to stay anymore."

"If you really want to go, we can cab to my sister's apartment," said Grace neutrally.

"If that's okay with you," I said.

"Okay," she added.

We said goodbye to everyone, then walked to a busy street to signal for a cab. After giving the driver her sister's address, Grace coiled into herself.

"Are you upset?" I said.

"I would have stayed longer, but it's fine," said Grace.

"I am sorry I wanted to go," I said. "I asked you if that was okay. We could have stayed longer if you had just told me, 'I want to stay.'"

"I didn't want you to be bored out of your mind waiting for me," said Grace. "But you know, if I can say something, I think part of the problem is your attitude. You can be snobby sometimes."

"I am not snobby," I said. "What makes you say that?"

"The different bands at The Ship, I just knew you were thinking, 'This is dumb,' like you're above that instead of trying to enjoy it for what it is," said Grace. "It's the same thing when we try to watch movies. It takes us an hour to find something to watch and you always seem to hate every movie."

"I am sorry all Hollywood movies are terrible," I said. "I am not going to watch, like, an Owen Wilson movie or something. Do you really want to watch that? Why would anyone want to watch that?"

"You know what I mean," said Grace. "You think everything is stupid.

"When you promote yourself on Facebook, you always post this half-serious bullshit, like, 'Here's this thing that I made for DIS magazine, you can look at it if you want, whatever, I don't care.' You're so afraid of people thinking that you take yourself seriously, even though you do. Why can't you be honest instead? Why can't you say, like, 'This is an art video that I made for a big publication, I worked hard on it and I am proud of it. I invite you to check it out.' Why can't you say something like that?"

"I don't know," I said. "I guess I don't have an answer to that."

The cab stopped on the side of the road. I paid our fare using the $20 bill that Grace's grandma had given me, hoping that maybe me paying for a cab for once would serve as a peace offering, but Grace didn't react.

22

The next morning, I woke up on a couch in Lindsay's living room, with Grace sleeping on the larger sofa across from me. I felt tired and lightly depressed, wanted a break from being around people. In Toronto, I had gotten so used to spending hours alone and living in relative seclusion that being constantly around people in Newfoundland felt like a kind of shock therapy. I was starting to miss my email inbox, wanted to do nothing for a while, maybe stare at my computer, browse Tumblr, feel satisfaction just from performing the repetitive action of scrolling, like a cat purring while kneading.

One problem was that I had told Grace I would spend the day with Lindsay and her visiting various relatives. After breakfast, I gathered my things and sat in the backseat of Lindsay's car. We spent most of the day travelling from one person's house to the next, spending about an hour in each location. One of Grace's uncles was a talented storyteller, but spoke with a heavy accent that was even more pronounced than Grace's grandfather's, giving his anecdotes a kind of weird, avant-garde feel. I couldn't understand most of his stories, could only latch onto a verb or a noun here and there. "Okay, so in this story, he's selling a vacuum cleaner to someone?" I thought. "And now he's being yelled at? Or he's in pain? Is that the punchline? Being in pain?"

Throughout the day, I was nice to Grace's relatives and managed, somehow, to maintain the appearance of being like-able, but could tell that I wasn't fully there, that I was losing the ability to engage psychologically with the present and needed to be alone for a while to recuperate.

After our last visit of the day, I sat in Lindsay's car and breathed a sigh of relief. I thought Lindsay was going to drop us off at her dad's house, but she mentioned wanting to make a quick stop by the Bath and Body Works inside the Avalon Mall first. "Oh god, I am so tired, I don't know if I can do this," I thought. "I don't know if I can be inside a mall."

Ten minutes later, we parked outside the shopping centre. Dragging my body towards the entrance, I imagined myself firing a flare gun to signal my emotional distress.

At Bath and Body Works, I looked around the store once and found nothing of interest. I exited the space and sat on a bench in the mall, feeling exhausted. Grace took her time, reading labels and weighing her options. Another difference between Grace and me was our approach to shopping. My strategy was to buy anything and then leave the store as quickly as possible while Grace's strategy was to carefully examine almost every item the store had to offer and then purchase only the best possible product for her needs, like she was trying to win at shopping.

Forty minutes passed. Seeing Grace and Lindsay exit Bath and Body Works, I thought, "Oh good, we can leave now," but then Lindsay proposed going to a jewellery store nearby to show her sister the engagement ring she was hoping Colin would purchase for her.

"He better propose to me soon," said Lindsay. "If I see one more person on Facebook announcing her engagement when she's been with her boyfriend for way less longer than I've been with Colin, I swear."

After showing Grace her favourite ring, Lindsay started talking to a sales assistant in the store. I stood next to Grace while she inspected the other engagement rings on display.

"This one's beautiful," said Grace, pointing out a gold ring. "Which one do you like?"

"I don't know," I said. "They're all the same."

"They're not all the same," said Grace. "Make an effort. You're an artist. You're supposed to like beautiful things."

"That doesn't mean I like dumb beautiful things," I said.

"What's dumb about an engagement ring?" said Grace.

"Nothing," I said. "I guess I don't like the wedding industry. They want you to think that if you don't spend a certain amount of money on a ring or whatever, then you don't love the person as much. That's why I don't like giant circus weddings. They just seem hollow to me."

"But it's your wedding," said Grace. "There's nothing wrong with spending a little money. You only get one."

"That's not what I mean," I said. "Just, forget it. I am tired. I am tired and I am grumpy and I don't want to fight."

"You started it," said Grace, looking displeased. "I don't know why you hate weddings."

"I don't hate weddings," I said. "I just don't want to feel like I am being bullied into buying ridiculous bullshit. Does it not count as a wedding if you don't have, like, dinner plates with the couple's names written in cursive on them?"

"That's a keepsake," said Grace. "You don't need it, but it can be something that the guests take home to remember the wedding."

"They're not going to forget a fucking wedding," I said.

"Don't take this the wrong way," said Grace, "but I wish you were more open with money. We probably make the same amount of money per year and you always spend way less than I do. Sometimes you go to ridiculous lengths to avoid taking the bus, just because it costs three dollars. Three fucking dollars."

"I know my money situation is not great, but I am doing my best with what I have," I said. "Also, there's a difference between your money and my money. You have a job, you know where your next paycheque is coming from. I rarely do. I always feel like money I spend today is money I won't have tomorrow. Plus, I've been broke the entire time we've been dating. You didn't know me back when I had a full-time job. I was less careful with money then."

"I don't know," said Grace. "When we go to restaurants, you never order enough food for yourself. You always end up eating from my plate."

"You offer," I said. "You offer me your food because you're going to throw it out anyway, so I eat it. You can't offer me food and then admonish me for saying yes. You can't have it both ways."

"Whatever," said Grace, who was starting to become emotional. "Sometimes I wonder if you're just happy living like that. It doesn't seem like you have any kind of plan for ever making money. I am not saying you need to be a billionaire, but it could be nice if you weren't on the verge of bankruptcy at all times."

"What do you think I am working on?" I said. "I really feel like you don't value enough what I do. You think I am just fucking around, but you can sell digital art the same way paintings are sold now. You can sell websites as art. And maybe it's a pipe dream to think I'll ever be able to live only through art, but what I know for sure is that the more established I get and the more visibility I have, the more opportunities I'll get. Maybe down the road I can convert that into some sort of teaching gig or something. Apparently, I don't hate teaching."

"Okay," said Grace. "That's fine, but it's just, I don't know. Other than art, it feels like you want nothing from life."

"Don't bash nothing," I said. "Wanting nothing from life is a perfectly valid option."

"Why would you want nothing?" said Grace.

"What's the alternative?" I said.

"I don't know," said Grace. "Living in a nicer space, having a dumb kid, putting money aside for when you're older, that kind of thing."

"I don't see it," I said.

"What do you mean, 'I don't see it?'" said Grace. "What kind of answer is that?"

"If I am honest, I am not sure I see any of that happening," I said. "It all sounds like a fucking nightmare to me. I don't know how to have normal life goals and do the art thing at the same time, especially when I am already struggling so much as an artist. I am sorry if this is disappointing to you, but I have no idea if I'll ever be stable. And part of me thinks that's fine. Part of me thinks maybe it's better that way."

23

The following afternoon, I stayed alone at Grace's dad's house while Grace went out for coffee with a friend from high school. I drank tea and stared at my laptop for several hours, which didn't feel nearly as good as how I had imagined it would. "Tea," I thought. "Wet plants," I thought. I felt bad about the fight with Grace, wanted to make things better, but I also knew that the best thing I could do at this moment was simply to allow time to pass.

"I just discovered this program through the City of Montreal that I am eligible for," read an email from Jane. "It's technically to help you start a business, but I am going to try applying with an art project. I would get paid minimum wage, full time, for the entire duration of the program. Earlier today, I was doing the math of how much I'd be getting per week and it seemed like a fortune to me. I'd be rich."

Browsing the internet, I read a news article on ArtNet, then stumbled on a blog post about "climate trauma" and "climate change anxiety," which was described as "a sense of helplessness in the looming shadow of climate change."

Later, in the evening, Grace and I received via email our invitations to the murder mystery dinner at Diane's house. The email said something about "voyaging aboard the Titanic" and instructed us to "dress elegantly." My character was a wealthy theatre director named Henry Higgins while Grace would be playing the role of my wife, Irene. After trying on several outfits for her character, none of which seemed entirely satisfying, Grace stumbled on her old prom dress in a closet and couldn't resist putting it on. The dress was black and red and extravagant-looking, something the Queen of Hearts from a deck of cards might have worn. "If I pin it in the back, it might fit," I overheard Grace tell her dad. "It's funny, I am having the opposite problem as everyone else. I can't fit into my old prom dress not because I've gained weight since then, but because I've lost some."

Two days passed. On the way to Diane's house, we stopped at a liquor store. Grace and I agreed to purchase a bottle of wine each, but then I caught Grace off-guard by paying for both at the register.

"Why didn't you let me buy one?" said Grace as we were coming out of the store.

"I am throwing money around so that you stop thinking that I am too careful with money," I said. "I am paying for everything from now on. It's the best kind of passive-aggressive revenge."

"Well, don't spend money if you don't have it," said Grace.

"I told you, money is stupid," I said.

About an hour later, in the living room at Diane's house,

Grace and I chatted with Ashlyn, Roberto, Andrea, Diane, Ben and Emily before dinner. Everyone was in costume, including Grace in her prom dress, me wearing a jacket I had borrowed from Walter, Diane sporting elaborate makeup and a long pearl necklace, and Roberto dressed in a dark grey tweed blazer and a sea captain hat. Sitting on a couch, I examined the label of the beer I was drinking, which claimed that one of its ingredients was "ancient iceberg water." "That's one way to solve global warming," I thought. "Turn the melting glaciers into beer."

"Sorry for my dishevelled appearance, folks," said Phil, emerging from a room. "I was just making la siesta before dinner. Right, Roberto?"

Roberto smiled politely.

"I'll be ready in about twenty minutes," said Phil.

We finished our drinks, then Phil asked us to move to the kitchen, where we sat at predetermined positions around the table. To set the mood, a television screen was showing an aquarium DVD on loop while computer speakers were playing the soundtrack of the movie Titanic. "Imagine yourself at sea," said Phil.

Ashlyn, who was wearing a black dress with gold trim, explained that she would be acting as master of ceremonies while Phil would handle food service. She welcomed everyone aboard the Titanic and asked the participants to introduce themselves one by one, starting with the captain.

"I am the captain," said Roberto. "Mister John. Edwards. I am a great captain."

Roberto wasn't a very good actor, making the delivery of his lines unintentionally over the top and very funny.

"Thank you for having us aboard your luxurious ship," said Ashlyn, who was laughing at Roberto's acting skills. "Tell us, what is the secret to being a good captain?"

"The key to being a captain," said Roberto before pausing briefly, "is being a leader. And taking good decisions. The bad decisions are the worst."

"Thank you, Mr. Captain," said Ashlyn. "Very informative. And to your left, we have?"

"Hi," said Andrea, who was wearing a black hat with a veil and a feather. "So I am Tessie Gibson. My invitation said that I was Miss Gibson's niece, that I was 'gorgeous-looking' and that I have problems controlling my impulses. Which is all true, so it shouldn't be that much of an acting challenge."

"And tell us, young lady, what do you want from life?" said Ashlyn.

"I want," said Andrea, "men. And tacos. Men and tacos."

"Men and tacos," said Ashlyn, laughing. "An astute answer. After all, who amongst us doesn't crave men and tacos once in a while? I sure do. Well, let's move on."

"I am Miss Gibson," said Diane with great conviction. Next to us, she felt like a professional actress with years of experience who had somehow ended up in a poorly directed children's play. "I am a wealthy heiress and a prominent figure within elite social circles. I am here to chaperone my niece Tessie and make sure she stays proper. No men and tacos for her."

"My aunt is the worst," said Andrea.

Next, Ben and Emily introduced themselves. Ben was a humble traveller from the lower classes while Emily was a rich widow with a Southern accent who had inherited her former husband's fortune.

"And finally, we have a couple on board," said Ashlyn.

"That's right," said Grace. "I am Irene Higgins and this is my husband, Henry. We are happily married."

"Isn't love beautiful?" said Ashlyn.

"It's the best," said Roberto.

"Mr. Higgins, I understand you are involved in theatre?" said Ashlyn.

"I am," I said. "I've produced plays all over the world."

"Anything we might have seen?" said Ashlyn.

"Yes," I said. "I directed a play called *The Matrix* about a man who realizes that reality is a simulation. Our special effects were cutting edge."

"Well, that sounds delightful," said Ashlyn. "Now, as you know, it's no coincidence that we are all gathered here tonight. There has been a murder on the *Titanic*, and everyone here is a suspect."

"A murder? On my ship?" said Roberto in an entertaining manner.

"Oh my," said Diane in full acting mode.

The victim, Ashlyn informed us, was a young man named Billy Peters, a worker on the ship who had been found dead a little after midnight. While Phil was serving the meal's first course, yellow pea soup, we completed an initial round of questions and answers, with each character reading a prepared cue card to reveal what he or she was doing at the time of the incident.

"I would never murder a man who works on my ship," said Roberto, improvising a little. "That would be against the code of the captain. The code of not killing."

"About an hour before the murder, I was out having a smoke," said Ben a few questions later, "and I am convinced that I saw Miss Tessie and young Billy holding hands while looking at the ocean."

"It's true," said Andrea. "Young Billy and I met through Tinder and became lovers, but he was nothing but a fun distraction for me. There are plenty of men in my life. I can't commit to just one."

"Tessie!" said Diane, reacting in mock outrage.

"I am sorry if my behaviour is upsetting you, my aunt," said Andrea, "but I can't help myself. I am burning with lust and passion."

Andrea banged on the table with her fist, making everyone laugh.

During the game's second chapter, it was revealed that young Billy wanted to pursue acting and that Andrea's character had also flirted with Ben's character as well as my character. Lastly, and more importantly, it was established that the sea captain was young Billy's biological father. His biological mother was Miss Gibson, who had had a romantic fling with the captain a long time ago, resulting in an undisclosed pregnancy.

"My aunt, I can't believe you would give me so much grief about being flirtatious with men," said Andrea, pretending to be upset, "when clearly, you've had your share of gentlemen visitors yourself."

"Now, now, Tessie, this was a different time," said Diane.

"No, Billy, my son," said Roberto, trying and failing to act devastated by the loss of his make-believe son. "Yo, I can't believe it. Oh my god."

In the final chapter, it was revealed that my character had accumulated important debts, as most of my plays had cost more to produce than they had generated in revenue. "What a surprise," said Ashlyn, directing the conversation. "Producing *The Matrix* in 1912 isn't cheap."

Then the group learned that young Billy had caught my character trying to steal a valuable painting from the sea captain's private quarters.

"My painting, I can't believe it," said Roberto. "You son of a bitch. That painting is worth so much money. That's why I brought it with me on my boat."

"I think what the captain is trying to say is that the painting is safe here because this ship can never sink," said Ashlyn, laughing. "It's great logic."

Everyone voted on who they believed the murderer to be. In a final twist, it was revealed that the true culprit was not my character, but Grace's. After being caught trying to steal the painting, my character had offered young Billy an important part in an upcoming play in exchange for his silence. Later, Grace's character had decided on her own to eliminate young Billy, as she felt she couldn't take the chance of him talking and ruining her husband's public reputation, despite their agreement.

"I can't believe you would kill for me," I said to Grace, smiling.

"I would kill for you," said Grace, smiling back. "Well, my character would kill for you. I would sacrifice something for you if it doesn't involve murdering someone. I am probably too short to be a killer. You can't have a 5' 2" killer. It just doesn't work."

With the game ending, we all thanked Phil for dinner and Diane insisted on taking photos of everyone in costume. Ben and Emily, who had hired a babysitter for the night, said goodbye and left while the rest of us sat around the living room, socializing. Around 2 a.m. Grace and I retreated to a bedroom downstairs, where we would be sleeping for the night.

"That was funny," I said.

"I know," said Grace. "I wasn't sure how a murder mystery was going to turn out, but I think we made something out of it."

"I think so too," I said. "Maybe we should replace partying in our lives with murder mysteries."

"Yeah," said Grace, laughing a little. "I am actually starting to feel shitty, but it has nothing to do with tonight. It's probably because I took Plan B the other day."

"I am sorry you had to take Plan B," I said. "And sorry we had a fight the other day. Sorry I was an asshole."

"That was a good fight," said Grace.

"I don't know if I meant what I said," I said. "My life is still such a work in progress, it's hard for me to know where I'll be in a few years. What I know for sure is that I love you and that I think I make way more sense as a person when you're around."

"I am glad you think that," said Grace. "My family likes you. I thought Dad was going to nitpick you, but he was fine with you pretty much right away. He didn't have anything bad to say, which was mind-blowing."

"I feel like we're not just dating anymore," I said. "It's bigger than that now. It's like you promoted me at some point, to Senior Boyfriend or something."

"I know," said Grace. "Though, if I am honest, I am not sure where we go from here."

"I've been thinking that maybe I should move back to Montreal," I said. "My financial situation is not great and I can't seem to find anything close to a real job in Toronto, so I have to do something. If I moved back, we could try living together, like that week where I was staying at your place. It would be cheap for both of us. I could pay back my credit card."

"Are you absolutely sure this is what you want?" said Grace.

"I think so, yeah," I said. "I didn't really accomplish what I wanted to in Toronto, but I am kind of at peace with that. It's almost like it's a good thing that I failed."

CHAPTER FOUR

Delusional Artist with Bad Full-time Job

01

What if art wasn't a career after all, but just a hobby I felt comfortable dumping infinite hours into, something I could never be bored of that solved the problem of what to do with my life?

02

I wasn't how sure how to tell people I had turned thirty. It felt like giving them bad news.

03

Cut myself while shaving and went to a job interview looking like I was recently attacked by a crab.

04

"They love the giant window," said Grace, who was curled into a ball on our living room couch. It was the third week of February and Grace and I were living together in a one-bedroom apartment on Saint-Laurent, near Beaubien. Our cats were staring out the living room window together, monitoring the backyard for squirrel activity like private detectives on a stakeout.

"It's like we've bought them a big screen TV," I said.

"Are you going to judge me if I order weed?" said Grace, raising her head. "I just feel so off today. I am really tempted to call my delivery guy."

"I am not going to tell you if it's a good idea or not," I

said. "You're a strong, independent woman. You can do what you want."

"I am so not," said Grace. "I am a weak, codependent woman."

"Come here, weaky," I said, forcing Grace to get up from the couch.

"Don't call me 'weaky,'" said Grace, laughing. "That's not a cute nickname."

"I was just kidding," I said. "Did you take Adderall this morning?"

"I did, twenty minutes ago," said Grace. "Still waiting for it to kick in."

Grace finally had a proper Adderall prescription, though was now half-trying to quit weed, as her new therapist had gotten mad at her for smoking regularly, telling her that she was "justifying" her consumption and didn't actually need weed to sleep at night. Adderall hadn't drastically overhauled Grace's personality, but it had made her more proactive in general, the kind of person who might click "Install immediately" instead of "Ask me later" when prompted by a computer for permission to install upgrades. From time to time, she would explode into sudden rampages of cleaning around the apartment, like her dad.

With the help of Adderall, Grace was trying to complete her physics course again. She had a different teacher this time around, a younger model less prone to mumbling, and though she seemed to be struggling less, the class still required her to put in a massive number of hours studying, completing assignments or watching physics videos on Khan Academy.

My productivity, like Grace's, was also trending upwards. Grace would let me have her Adderall "leftovers," and though

I was trying to avoid growing dependent on the drug, Adderall was clearly helping me get more work done by turning my brain into an electrical storm, what I imagined transforming into a werewolf would feel like.

My main problem, now, wasn't productivity, but time. Shortly after moving back to Montreal, I had started a new, not particularly well-paid full-time job as a graphic designer for a company that offered SEO services to universities, colleges and private schools, helping them improve their rankings on Google. To do so, the company published several times per week short, generic blog articles that weren't meant to be read and contained targeted keywords and links that didn't go anywhere, on websites that barely seemed to exist.

This generated money, somehow.

At work, I would sit in front of my computer and then waste away like a snowman melting in the sun. My plan was to hopefully pile up money for a while and then quit this job, though I still hadn't determined how much money I should pile, or how long it would take me to pile it. As a whole, my strategy of saving money in order to be able to afford being un-employed again felt kind of like putting quarters into an arcade video game machine, in that it would probably only buy me a finite number of lives before I would have to get a job again.

"Girl, you're crazy," said Grace, addressing my cat. Battle was frantically digging through the cat litter she shared with Tom-Tom, performing a kind of fracking operation.

"She's just picking up your cat's slack," I said. "He never buries his poop. He just leaves it there."

"Tom-Tom means well," said Grace. "He just never got his cat training from other cats. He never learned how to be a cat."

"He's like a special needs cat," I said.

185

"He's not a special needs cat," said Grace defensively. "Don't call him that. He's just a late bloomer. A handsome, special late bloomer."

"I was kidding," I said.

"You were asleep when I got home last night," said Grace, "so I don't think I told you this, but when I took him to the vet yesterday, they weighed him and he was twenty-six pounds. I am going to have to put him on a diet."

"You should just start giving him Adderall," I said. "Maybe that would help him lose weight."

"Yeah," said Grace. "Or maybe he would finally feel motivated enough to clean himself."

05

Having a full-time job meant having a fixed schedule and getting up early every morning, usually before Grace, an interesting reversal of our previous routine in which I would sleep in while she would go to work. The company I worked for employed about twenty people who shared an open floor studio. Every day, I skillfully avoided opportunities to get to know my new co-workers, treated work like it was some sort of witness protection program. I didn't want to make friends, didn't want to tell my co-workers about my life, didn't want to become emotionally attached to this new job. I wanted my co-workers to have low expectations of me, so that I wouldn't stand out, would never be promoted, would be able to quit whenever I felt like it.

I was trying to limit my exposure to this job, like looking at the sun through a pinhole in a shoebox.

During the day, the studio was usually quiet, as most people had headphones on to focus on their work tasks. Every two hours or so, the lead graphic designer, Fabio, who was originally from Argentina, would get up, crack his spine like he was about to throw a disk at an Olympic event, then sit back down. From time to time, the owner and head manager, who was named Jean-Marc, would come out of his office and complain that we weren't having enough "fun."

"Come on, work doesn't have to be boring," he would say.

"Deadlines," he would say a few sentences later.

To encourage us to have more "fun," Jean-Marc would sometimes buy us lunch on Fridays, resulting in an awkward hour during which the team would sit around a table in the office's only meeting room and eat delivery Chinese food. Jean-Marc would supervise these lunches, preventing us from going back to work until we had met an unspecified quota of personal interactions.

"So, what is everyone doing this weekend?" said Jean-Marc during a lunch hour. "Daniel, what are you doing?"

"I don't know," I said.

"You don't know?" said Jean-Marc. "No plans? Don't like going out? Stay at home and stare at the walls? Come on, you're still young, you don't have kids. You can go out and party. Live the life! I would if I was you."

"I'll think of something," I said.

"What does your wife think of that?" said Jean-Marc.

"Oh," I said. "Grace, the person I listed as my emergency contact number, is my girlfriend. We live together, but we're not married."

"I'd lock her down fast if I was you," said Jean-Marc. "Trust me, you don't realize how good you have it."

"That's probably true," I said. "I'll tell her you pressured me to propose. She might like that, actually."

"Hey, I am here to help," said Jean-Marc, smiling.

06

Every office felt like the same office.

07

In many ways, living with Grace was harder than dating long distance. Though I didn't think we were doing bad, it felt like something had changed since Newfoundland. We were having sex less frequently, were starting to function less like lovers and more like indoor pets for one another. We were trying to be equals, would take turns doing the dishes, take turns buying cat food, take turns at everything. If one of us said, "I took out the garbage," it vaguely implied that the other owed one action of similar value, a kind of competition in which the winner was allowed to be passive-aggressive with the loser.

We were trying to be equals, but who was the most equal?

08

After growing tired of walking to work every day, I gave up and purchased a bus pass for the first time in two years. My version of "wealth" was being able to take public transport every day like a rich person.

09

The cats were using an empty cardboard box to play a version of peekaboo that always ended with one cat trying to claw the other's face. Tom-Tom was losing.

10

"Bachelor party!" shouted Derek while laughing, his mouth filled with black pepper and lime chips. It was Saturday night and a week before Roberto and Ashlyn's wedding. Grace, Val, Andrea and Jane had decided to throw Ashlyn an impromptu bachelorette party, leaving Derek, Roberto, Elliot and me at my apartment, drinking beers or leftover white rum mixed with mango juice, wondering what to do. No one had planned or even discussed throwing Roberto a bachelor party, as it hadn't seemed like a serious possibility until now.

"What do you want to do?" said Derek. "It's your night, you tell us."

"I don't know," said Roberto, who seemed amused by the idea of a bachelor party, kept grinning whenever anyone said the words "bachelor party" aloud. "We could go to Exxxotica."

"I don't know," said Derek. "The strippers at Exxxotica are kind of old and not that attractive. There are all these sketchy old guys roaming around. It's not a good place."

"Oh," said Roberto, sounding disappointed.

"My band once played a show at the space above Exxxotica," said Elliot. "It was quite disturbing. There were mirrors every-where. Poles where there shouldn't be poles."

"We should take mushrooms, then go to Exxxotica," I said.

"That's a terrible idea," said Derek. "Where would we even get mushrooms?"

"I have mushrooms," said Elliot.

"You do?" said Derek.

"Yes, back at my place," said Elliot. "I'd be happy to share. My treat for your special night, little man."

"I am down," said Roberto, grinning.

A few minutes later Elliot left my apartment. While waiting for him to return, I asked Roberto how the wedding preparations were going and he replied that he wanted his wedding to be simple and "relaxing," by which he probably meant "not stressful." Derek searched Soundcloud on my computer and put on a party mix by Ryan Hemsworth, trying to get us "into it," though I couldn't tell if "being into it" was something I wanted or not. Since I had started drinking again, I hadn't felt the need to drink to feel less anxious around people as much, and as a result, hadn't gotten wasted in a while. "Party mode" now felt to me like some sort of remote and exotic destination, like Japan.

Twenty minutes passed. Rejoining our group, Elliot handed Roberto a small Ziploc bag and Derek, Roberto and I ate a handful of mushrooms. Roberto told the group a story about his first visit to Montreal, back in 2009. At the time, he didn't know anyone living here, or much about Canada in general. After reading on a website that the Jean-Talon Market had a strong Latino community, he had travelled there hoping to find work. Asking around, he had been told by someone to show up at 6 a.m. outside a metro station in Montreal-Nord. The next day, he had waited in line with other people, some Mexicans, but also some Cubans, Chileans and two people from El Salvador. After giving his name to someone, he had been instructed to climb into a van that didn't have windows. In the van, he had felt afraid that he was being deported for having tried to secure work without a work permit, but then a few hours later, the van had reached a farm somewhere outside of Montreal, where he was told to put on heavy boots, wash salad and trim cucumbers. The other men, who were all older, faster and more experienced than him, had refused to socialize with him, as they had assumed, for mysterious reasons, that he was Canadian, a confusion that was only a cleared up the next day after the men overheard Roberto swear in Spanish. From that point on, the other men were nice to him, often giving him advice or sharing with him their life stories. Most of the money these men made, Roberto learned, would go to their families back home, and some had come to Canada seeking asylum, trying to evade death threats. One time, immigration officers had made a surprise visit to inspect the farm. Someone had shouted "la migra" and Roberto had had to run into some nearby woods along with the other men, spending the night there hiding behind a tree.

Around midnight, Derek said, "We should go," and Roberto, who was already fairly drunk, had difficulty putting on his winter boots. Walking down Parc Avenue a few minutes later, Roberto spotted a dog tied to a pole near a convenience store across the street. Wanting to pet the dog, an inebriated but high-energy Roberto crossed the street in a cavalier manner, apparently not realizing that he was running. This terrified the dog, which reacted by barking loudly and aggressively at him.

"Poor dog, you just scared the shit out of it," said Derek, laughing.

"Yo, I just wanted to pet it," said Roberto.

"He's growling at you," said Derek. "Look at him. He's in full-on attack mode. He's ready to pounce."

"I still want to be his friend," said Roberto.

"You can be friends with other dogs," said Derek. "This one needs his space right now. Come on."

Several streets later, we reached Exxotica and went in. The stamp at the door was a drawing of a female silhouette in a sitting position, as if doing yoga. I stood in the back next to Elliot and observed the dancer onstage. After a few minutes, I began losing awareness of my surroundings and focusing too much on the man in front of me's neck tattoo, which made me realize that the mushrooms had begun to kick in.

A disoriented-looking Roberto asked where the bathrooms were located and Derek volunteered to accompany him.

"Why are we here again?" I said to Elliot, shouting over the music coming from the sound system.

"I am not sure," said Elliot. "This is quite strange. So how do you feel about being back in Montreal?"

"It's good," I said. "It's like a second honeymoon or something. Being away from it made me appreciate it more."

"That's why I love going on tour," said Elliot. "I always come back with a fresh perspective."

"I wish I had more free time," I said, "but right now, I am stuck with a full-time job for a while. It's hard to sit at a computer all day and then come home at night and feel like working on my own things. Realistically, I don't know how I am supposed to be a full-time employee, an artist and a boyfriend all at the same time. I feel like I can only be a shitty employee, a nonexistent artist and an insufficient boyfriend."

"Don't be too hard on yourself," said Elliot. "You don't seem to be doing too bad to me. You have your life together much more than a lot of people that I know who are 30."

"I am 30 now," I said.

"You are?" said Elliot.

"Yeah," I said. "My birthday was earlier this year. I was still in Toronto, getting ready to move back."

"Oh," said Elliot. "Well, happy birthday."

Returning from the bathroom with Derek, Roberto complained that the bar was too noisy, that there was too much activity and that the dancer was making him feel "nervous."

Elliot proposed leaving, which everyone agreed was a good idea.

Less than ten minutes after entering, we regrouped out-side of Exxotica. Derek said, "Well, that was stupid," and laughed. We decided to go to Elliot and Jane's loft and began walking east. Because of the mushrooms, my thought process was starting to feel long-winded and elaborate, like a Rube Goldberg machine with hundreds of individual moving parts. On Fairmount, I recognized Fabio from work, who was walking in the opposite direction. As we crossed paths, we exchanged head nods and polite smiles.

"Do you know this guy?" said Derek.

"We work together," I said. "Thank god he didn't want to stop and have a conversation. I feel like I might have asked him if he has a neck tattoo and if I can stare at it for a while."

"Do you think he realized you were on mushrooms?" said Derek.

"No, I think I held it together," I said. "That was a very pro-fessional head nod. Maybe it was too professional. That's out of character for me, now that I think about it."

"You could make up for it by running after him all crazy like Roberto with the dog," said Derek.

"Maybe I should," I said.

A few minutes later, we reached Elliot and Jane's loft and were greeted at the door by Jane's golden retriever, who was wearing an elegant red scarf and small black socks that made her look like a ballerina. "Hi Dora," I said, taking off my winter jacket and then hugging her, my sweater quickly becoming covered in fur. The dog licked my hands. Dora was originally Jane's family dog and had been transferred to Jane after her parents' move to Mexico City. Petting the dog made me picture my Christmas two years before, taking care of Dora during the holidays while Jane was out of town visiting her family. I remembered taking Dora out for a walk on Christmas morning and feeling unsettled by how deserted and eerie Montreal looked, making me feel like I was in some post-apocalyptic film, like that movie in which Will Smith is the only human left alive in a large, abandoned metropolis. "What was that movie called again?" I thought, and then couldn't remember. "I am Will Smith," I thought.

I sat on the floor by the main window, with Dora lying next to me. The loft was decorated with plants, Christmas lights, haphazard music gear, a moon calendar, crystals, two Aztec sculptures and a few prints Jane had made. On a black table next to me were two books, *Ways of Seeing* by John Berger and something called *Animal Wisdom: Harness the Power of Animals to Liberate your Spirit*.

Roberto, Derek and I ingested mushrooms again. Sitting on the floor and staring out the window, I participated in the group conversation for a little while, then rested my head on Dora's stomach and concentrated on the sound of her breathing.

My mind became filled with colourful emojis.

11

The following afternoon, Grace and I were both hungover and decided to stay in, order food and watch episodes of *Master-Chef* on a pirate website. On my screen, Gordon Ramsay talked about "elevating" a dish and said things like "acidity" and "huge advantage." "Acidity is a huge advantage," I thought. I felt guilty for wasting an entire day that I could have used to work on things, but was tired and couldn't focus very well. Trying to think, I could hear synapses inside my brain stretching themselves and then snapping like overextended rubber bands.

Over text message, Ashlyn told Grace that after returning home from Elliot and Jane's loft the night before, Roberto, still drunk, had vomited in the bathroom and then decided, for some reason, to call 911, thinking he was suffering from alcohol poisoning. Apparently, he had been a little too dramatic on the phone, as an ambulance, a cop car and a fire truck had all showed up at his apartment about twenty minutes later, expecting to find someone whose life was in danger.

"I don't understand the weird ads on this website," I said, looking for a link for the next episode of *MasterChef*.

"What do you mean?" said Grace.

"I mean, whenever you click on anything, you get a popup for a game called *League of Angels*, or it tells you to install something called Mac Cleaner, or some guy in a video says that he wants to teach you one simple trick to make money," I said. "What is that? What's *League of Angels*?"

"They're just ads," said Grace

"I know, I just mean, why doesn't, like, Walmart buy ads on this thing?" I said. "I know it's a pirate website, but they probably get a crazy amount of traffic. Does the guy who wants to teach me one simple trick really have that much money that he can afford to buy all the ads on here?"

"I don't know," said Grace. "Maybe they can't sell ads to real companies because they're a pirate website. Maybe that's why all the ads are sketchy."

"Maybe I should buy an ad on there," I said. "I am here to teach you one simple trick to never have any money."

12

On Monday morning, I sat in the meeting room usually reserved for eating Chinese food awkwardly to attend a meeting that Jean-Marc had scheduled regarding the Higher Education Network, a website the company had launched as a side project a few months prior to my arrival. The goal of the Network, according to Jean-Marc, was to build an audience of students, which our clients could then advertise their programs to. So far, the Network had failed to create any traction, probably because the only content it offered was a steady output of generic blog posts about nothing.

"What I really like," Jean-Marc told everyone, "is these guys. Buzzfeed."

Up on the projector, Jean-Marc brought up Buzzfeed's Facebook page and showed us individual posts, all of which had many likes and comments.

"The content is light and funny," Jean-Marc said, highlighting a post from Buzzfeed's Facebook page. "That's what I want. The Buzzfeed of Higher Education. That's our vision for the Network. We need to rethink our content strategy. Right now, we're not getting any engagement. No likes, no retweets, nothing."

"So you're saying that our content," said Anish, a shy and nervous content manager originally from India, "is bad?"

Anish's accidental inflection reminded me of Teddy, my former South Korean student who had successfully argued in a debate that global warming was "bad."

"Yes," said Jean-Marc. "It needs to be more dynamic. Maybe we can pull some content from other websites. We continue posting our regular blogs, which our students enjoy, but we also create short entries about new TED talks that we think our audience would like, or topical events. Educational content, but that's also fun."

"Okay," said Anish, who didn't sound okay.

"We're going to have to redesign the site as well," said Jean-Marc. "Or maybe not redesign, but tweak. Fabio, I'd like to give this assignment to Daniel. I want to see what the new guy can do. Trial by fire! Daniel, I want to see something that's less conservative. We need a visual identity that's punchier."

"Like Buzzfeed," I said.

"Like Buzzfeed," repeated Jean-Marc.

13

At Citizen Vintage, Grace tried on a dress for Ashlyn and Roberto's wedding reception and ended up feeling self-conscious about her body. Wanting to be supportive, I said, "I love your body, I would laminate your body," but that didn't seem to help anything.

14

A repairman stopped by our apartment to fix a leaky faucet in our bathroom. Seeing a stranger walk in, my cat immediately ran into the bedroom to hide under the bed while Tom-Tom went up to the man to calmly request food. "Way to defend the house against intruders, guys," I said. "Great job. You're killing it."

15

"It was surprisingly poignant," said Grace of Ashlyn and Roberto's wedding ceremony. We were sitting in a bus on our way to a restaurant in Old Montreal and she was showing me pictures on her phone. The ceremony had been held in the downtown offices of a notary, with Grace serving as an official witness. In one picture, Ashlyn was sitting on an office chair, wearing a plain white dress and holding a bouquet of flowers, looking bored. In another, Roberto, sporting a black tie and a jacket, was standing next to a whiteboard on which someone had drawn a heart with a marker and written the couple's names inside it.

"Ashlyn read her vows in English and in Spanish," Grace added. "Or at least she tried to, it was both the best and worst Spanish I've ever heard. I was tearing up in the stupid office, though I tear up for everything, so I don't think that was a shock to anyone. The whole thing wasn't very wedding-like, like they didn't say 'in sickness and in health' and all of that, but I still thought it was beautiful and romantic."

"So she didn't do the thing at the end where she throws the flowers?" I said.

"No. I ended up getting the flowers, but I didn't catch them or anything," said Grace. "Ashlyn just gave them to me, probably because I was the only bachelorette there. Except maybe for the receptionist."

"Maybe the receptionist will be getting married next," I said.

About thirty minutes later, we arrived at Le Garde-Manger, where the wedding reception was taking place. Grace peeked into the kitchen, trying to see if celebrity chef Chuck Hughes, who owned the restaurant, was present.

"I wonder if he's going to be the one preparing our food tonight," she said.

"You can ask," I said. "Maybe you can get him to come out and scream at you like Gordon Ramsay."

"Not all celebrity chefs yell at people," said Grace. "It's not a prerequisite."

We crossed the room to go chat with Ashlyn and Roberto, who were talking with Ashlyn's mom and a couple who seemed to be Roberto's parents. I hugged Roberto and said, "Congratulations," and meant it. As we broke the hug, I thought about how this wedding seemed much more real to me than any "real wedding" I had attended in the past. For one, it had a concrete purpose, which was to allow Roberto to become a Canadian citizen, be able to work here legally, struggle less in life.

Roberto introduced me to his dad, a mild-mannered businessman in his forties named Rafael who spoke English well enough to be understood. Rafael told me a story about Roberto, how he was terrible at sports growing up, though had a knack for ending up on winning teams. Back in Mexico, Roberto had a box full of gold medals and trophies that he had won as a child despite spending a majority of the games sitting on various benches.

"That's funny," I said. "I also still have an old medal that I won playing sports as a kid."

"No way," said Roberto, which made me picture him and I wearing our childhood gold medals at the same time, feeling powerful together.

A voice behind me called my name. I turned around and realized that Jane and Elliot were both standing behind me, smiling.

"Oh," I said, hugging Jane. "Hey."

"I didn't want to surprise-hug you," said Jane. "I was afraid you might head-butt me by accident."

"That was probably wise," I said.

"Sorry I've been so busy since you moved back," said Jane.

"I've just been working a lot more as a nanny. Some days I have to be there at 6 a.m. It's been messing up my lack of schedule."

Jane laughed a little.

"It's okay," I said. "I am happy you're here now."

"Me too," said Jane. "Anyway. We need to talk. I have news."

Jane began telling me about a "networking dinner" she had attended a few months before. "I got invited to it for some reason," she said. "It was very business-y, so I felt out of my element. 80% of it seemed totally crazy to me. The other 20% was alright, though I am probably including the free meal in the 20%."

At the dinner, Jane explained, she had met someone who works for Eastern Bloc, a centre for contemporary art. Recently, this person had reached out to her by email, inviting her to submit a proposal for an exhibit that would be presented as part of an ongoing series curated by the centre. Jane wanted us to show our work together. She specified that the person she had been in been contact with was looking to fill an unforeseen opening in late April, meaning we would have to act fast.

"What do you think?" said Jane.

Without hesitating, I said, "Yes," and then, "Let's go for it." Jane replied, "Great," and smiled. An intense feeling of dread bored its way through me. I wasn't sure what material I was going to show or how I was going to make this work, but I felt that having a concrete deadline would force me to push something, anything out. The worst-case scenario, I thought, was my half of the show turning out to be a trainwreck, some sort of half-assedly thought-out semi-vision thing, but then this would only make Jane's work look better by comparison.

"This is going to be amazing," said Jane. "What should we call it?"

"What should we call what?" I said.

"The show," said Jane.

"Oh," I said. "I don't know."

"Well, it's still early," said Jane. "We'll think of something."

"If we can't think of anything, we can just call it, 'Memory,'" I said. "It works with everything."

About ten minutes passed. I sat down at a table next to Grace, across from Val and Andrea. Grace ordered a Bloody Mary from a short-haired waitress. Ashlyn's mom, who was holding a glass of white wine and looked exhilarated, approached our table.

"So, girls," said Diane. "Ashlyn was the first one of your group to get married. Who's going to be next?"

Diane smiled. She knew her question would make Andrea, Val and Grace uncomfortable, but hadn't been able to resist asking it. No one answered, and after several seconds of a powerful silence that seemed to threaten to devour the entire room, Grace rescued everyone by blurting out, "My sister."

"Oh yeah," said Andrea. "It'll be Lindsay for sure."

"I can't believe Colin still hasn't proposed to her," said Grace. "Lindsay is so eager to say yes. She probably says yes to him in her sleep."

"I don't want to sound pessimistic, but I don't know how or if I am ever going to get there," said Andrea.

"I wouldn't be too worried if I was you," said Diane. "Look at you, you're such a pretty little thing. Of course you'll find someone."

"No, I know," said Andrea. "I am great, it's everyone else that's the problem."

Sitting at another table, Roberto's dad began tapping his wineglass with a knife. Once he had the room's attention, he got up, thanked everyone for being so friendly and hospitable and then wished the newlyweds a long and happy marriage. Taking advantage of the interruption, Ashlyn decided to speak next. She thanked us all for coming and then added, as a joke, that she had only married Roberto because he had a "cool last name" and a "great hairline," which wouldn't be receding anytime soon. Roberto spoke last. "I can't believe," he said, grinning massively, what the birth of a star in outer space probably looked like. "Thank you for coming. This is huge. You are the best. Everyone is the best."

16

"Ashlyn's mom is such a party mom," said Grace in the cab on our way home. "She got way too drunk again tonight. At one point, I was going to the bathroom and she sort of cornered me. She asked me if I thought you were 'the one.'"

"What did you tell her?" I said.

"Well," said Grace, smiling. "All I said was, 'I hope so.'"

17

The month of March looked like a computer screen to me, with entire days sacrificing themselves like kamikazes, leaving only a hole in my memory. Except for the office, I avoided going out entirely, spending all my time at home working on things and abusing Grace's drug prescription, making me feel like time itself was on Adderall. Grace usually stayed in with me, putting in many hours studying physics and solving problems for class.

During this period, I began wondering if my approach was all wrong, if a smart person in my position would instead choose to concentrate on having a job and making money, give up art entirely, give up on social media, marry Grace, become nothing, "the Original Face." I felt frustrated that work wasn't progressing how I wanted it to, but then I realized that I was taking everything too seriously, wasn't having fun anymore. "Okay, I am going to try a new method," I thought. "From now on, I am only going to pursue what I think is fun. My stupidest ideas are usually my best anyway."

Eventually, I hit a breakthrough by revisiting the many abandoned or half-finished projects that were lying around on my hard drive. I completely overhauled a video by changing the focus and presentation, cutting several elements and playing with the order until everything fell into a place, a process that felt a little like trying to solve a 3,000-piece jigsaw puzzle, one whose final image was possibly my own insanity.

"How do I elevate this piece?" I thought, pretending that my video was a dish on *MasterChef*.

"Acidity," I thought.

"One thing that's annoying with Adderall is that it's a diuretic," said Grace, interrupting my thought process. "When I have an exam, I have to pee right before. By the time it's over, I am, like, half-crouched in my chair trying to solve complicated equations and I can't wait to finish so that I can go to the bathroom and pee again. It's stupid what I have to endure just to pass physics."

18

Had a dream in which I clicked on a hyperlink and it led me directly into another brain.

19

"I am so ready to ditch post-internet art," typed Eloise on Facebook Chat about ten minutes later. "That whole scene is just a massive circle jerk. Post-internet is dead. Fuck Brad Troemel."

"I honestly don't know why people are still calling it 'post-internet,'" I typed. "I can't think of a single person who doesn't think that term is embarrassing."

"I don't want to be a post-anything anymore," typed Eloise. "I want to be a pre-something. Like 'pre-cyborg art.'"

"Pre-cyborg art," I typed. "That would be a good slogan for your magazine. 'The best cyborg art from around the world.'"

"The other day, I went to this show called *Best, xoxo* and everything about it, from the poster with the bad '90s fonts to the pieces on display just seemed so incredibly annoying," typed Eloise. "It was the kind of work I probably would have felt excited about two or three years ago, except now it just seemed empty and vapid to me."

"Maybe it's the laws of diminishing returns," I typed. "The more you dabble in art, the more impossible you are to please."

"It's more than that," typed Eloise. "The show was supposed to be about 'emotional labour' and this book called *The Commercialization of Human Feeling*, but some of it was literally just a black-and-white drawing of an iPhone with a message on the screen that says 'Fuck u.' I looked at the iPhone and I thought 'Fuck u' and it seemed like the drawing and me at least agreed on something. Also, I couldn't believe how many art bros were at that. I had this thought at one point, that I should go around the room and collect a man tax. If I find you objectively terrible, you have to give me money."

"That's funny," I typed.

"I am also starting to get pissed off at the way people brand themselves on social media," typed Eloise. "It's such a sad practice. It could be a storyline in *Les Misérables*. That's how sad it is."

"I hate how anything I do or don't do on social media feels

like a type of branding," I typed. "It's like a Zen koan. 'How do you escape an inescapable net?'"

"I don't know if you've ever read David Foster Wallace," typed Eloise, "but he has this essay where he talks about television and people who have been marketed to all their lives. We're even worse than that. We're not just being marketed to nonstop, we've been given the tools to market ourselves. We live in a dystopia of marketing. Social media is a weapon. If ISIS really wanted to fuck with America, they would change their name to 'McDonalds.'"

"McDonalds' stock price plummets as U.S. Army sends more troops to Iraq to battle McDonalds," I typed.

"I don't know what to do about any of this," typed Eloise. "I guess leaving New York is a good start. I am leaving New York at the end of May."

"For real?" I typed.

"Yeah," typed Eloise. "It finally happened. I am almost out of money, plus I probably need to exit the country again, plus other problems. It's time. Before I leave, I want to put together a group show at Blindside. Do you think you and Jane would be able to come to New York for a few days to be a part of this? I'd love to show her work and yours."

"Let me ask Jane, but that sounds good to me," I typed.

"Great," typed Eloise. "I can handle all the legwork and promotion and everything. It's funny, I never promote dudes, but I am going to have to make an exception for you."

"I am honoured," I typed.

"Yeah," typed Eloise. "Don't fuck it up."

I surprised myself by delivering a shockingly competent redesign proposal for the Higher Education Network to Jean-Marc, who nodded and said, "Yes," and, "Great work." Later, Jean-Marc, Anish and Fabio all commented on my design to make it worse and then we proceeded to implement that version.

Walking back home from work, I recognized Grace from afar. She was standing on the corner of Parc and Van Horne and having a conversation with someone. Though my first thought was, "She's great at talking," I realized, getting closer, that she wasn't calmly chatting with a random stranger, but instead was having an argument with him.

"I don't appreciate you talking to me like this," I overheard her say.

"Talking to you like what?" the stranger said.

"All threatening," said Grace.

"I am not threatening you, I am just talking to you," the stranger said in a clearly threatening manner.

The person she was arguing with, I saw, was Michael the bike thief.

"Hey," I said, stepping in between them. "Leave her alone."

"In a good way," I almost wanted to add. "Leave her alone, in a good way."

"We're just talking," said Michael. "All I am saying is that we should be friends. Why would you be against that?"

"You don't even know what friends are," said Grace. "You have zero friends. Zero. Friends. Zero. Friends."

She repeated the words "Zero friends" while forming the number zero with her left index finger and thumb.

"She doesn't want to talk to you," I said, using the closest thing I had to a firm tone. "Just leave her alone."

Michael, who was taller than me, looked in my direction. I sensed my body becoming more alert, as if a smoke detector was now going off inside my head. I felt comically miscast trying to play the role of Grace's protector, couldn't help thinking that anyone else, even Tom-Tom, would have been a better choice for this part. Though Michael's body language was communicating frustration, it didn't seem like his anger had anything to do with Grace or me. He was simply angry because his life was his life. "He should be a wrestler on television," I thought.

After a few seconds of silence, Michael abruptly pushed my shoulder with his right hand, catching me off-guard. "Hey, hey, hey," Grace shouted quickly while I fell back a few steps. "What's wrong with you?"

Before I could react, Grace grabbed my arm and made me walk with her back towards our apartment. Michael stood on the corner and didn't follow us.

"Stupid piece of shit," said Grace.

"If you see him again and he tries to talk to you, let me know immediately," I said.

"What are you going to do?" said Grace.

"Something," I said. "I'll do something."

"Don't do anything stupid," she said.

22

Bored at work, I replayed in my head the incident with Michael the bike thief. I thought about how Grace, in the past, had often stayed in relationships despite being unhappy, trying to convince herself that she didn't deserve better. If she was unhappy with me and I became just another deranged jerk in her life, I thought, would I even realize it? "Deranged jerk boyfriend who brings her cupcakes from art shows," I thought.

23

"*Pure Reality / The Original Face* features new works by Jane Hatherley and Daniel Kerry," read the website for our show. "Hatherley's section, *Pure Reality*, presents videos and installations that speak to the artist's yearning for visceral experiences and true emotional exchanges in an increasingly digital world, forcing the spectator to reconsider the way we interact with technology and proving that tech doesn't have to be devoid of warmth. Kerry's side, *The Original Face*, offers a selection of animated GIFs, plus three narrative videos made using glitch art and video game footage. The videos can be viewed in any order, each seeking the 'Original Face.' In a culture obsessed with selfies and identity, what is the Original Face?"

24

"Power cords rule my life," I thought, setting up before the show.

25

"I can't believe this is happening," said Jane, who was wearing a dark purple dress and earrings shaped like hands. "Seriously, I can't even look." It was the opening night of our exhibit and I was feeling on edge, making me yearn for some sort of gadget that could collect my anxiety all into one place, a kind of modified diva cup maybe.

"This is great," said Elliot, trying to be supportive. "So many people here."

"Everything seems under control, I just don't know if I can be here right now," said Jane. "Part of me wants to hide under a pile of jackets and wait until everyone is gone and it's safe for me to leave."

Turning around, I saw that Roberto was studying the wall of animated GIFs in my section, an installation I had titled *You Look at the Glitch Until You Become the Glitch*. "Wow," he said to himself. It didn't seem like a "wow" because he didn't know what to say, but a "wow" because he was impressed. Each GIF featured a unique, hand-captured glitch that achieved a kind of visual sublime, encouraging the viewer to look at several repetitions of the same GIF as a way of "entering" it. Staring at the same GIF over and over again, I thought, could have the same effect as repeating a mantra in your head, allowing you to temporarily reach a deeper plane of consciousness. Every GIF came from a different 3D world and was presented with a physical label suggesting a loose interpretation, titles like *Work Life*, *Dream Box*, *Ego Death*, *Ego Heaven*, *Zen Mess*, *Emotional Abyss*, *Animal Wisdom* and *Megatrends 2010*.

One GIF was titled Memory.

In a separate room located nearby, three videos I had made were supersized by a projector and playing on loop over an entire wall, each entry exploring the concept of the "Original Face" from a different perspective. Facing the screen was a beanbag I had customized by digitally printing glitch motifs onto a fabric.

"This is all super weird but really great," said Grace. "It might sound stupid, but I forget that you're talented sometimes."

"I am happy you like it," I said, smiling.

"Okay, Elliot and I are going to step outside to smoke weed," said Jane.

"I'll come," said Grace. "I don't care if my therapist yells at me for smoking weed. It'll make her feel useful."

A few minutes later, Elliot, Jane, Grace, Roberto, Ashlyn and I all stood in a semi-circle in an alley outside the space, sharing weed. We chatted for a while, then I realized that the drug was hitting me harder than I thought it would. I zoned out, found myself focusing on Grace's nose and then on Elliot's nose, imagining the noses detaching themselves from their faces, challenging one another to a duel, a kind of sword fight.

"Grace, I completely forgot to tell you," said Ashlyn. "Congratulations on passing physics."

"Thank you," said Grace. "I did it! My final mark wasn't even that bad. I was so relieved when I saw my grade and I realized that I hadn't failed. I can finally apply to physical therapy."

"That's so great," said Ashlyn.

"Whoa, look at the moon tonight," said Jane, pointing at the sky. "It's so bright and badass."

"You're right," said Elliot. "It's like it's on steroids."

Everyone looked up. After a few seconds of silence, it dawned on me that we were finally doing it, were finally all observing the moon together, though I couldn't find a way to speak.

26

"With their exhibit *Pure Reality / The Original Face,* Montreal-based artists Daniel Kerry and Jane Hatherley undertake a spiritual quest for the digital era," read the opening paragraph of a short, largely positive article in the arts section of a mainstream local newspaper. "At times wistful, at times introspective and at times subtly funny, the duo's opening at Eastern Bloc was packed with fans, friends, fellow artists and curious onlookers alike. Introducing two creators from the internet generation."

27

Remembering my life according to what was on my computer screen at the time, thinking things like "The year *Diablo II* came out" instead of "2000."

28

A kind of capitalism that didn't involve enslaving your users.

29

"Do you have a minute?" I said, knocking on the door to Jean-Marc's office.

"Of course!" said Jean-Marc, who, as far as I could tell, didn't seem to be doing anything. "What's on your mind?"

"I'd just like to show you something," I said, handing him a copy of the newspaper. Though I wasn't sure this was a good idea, I had decided to show Jean-Marc the newspaper article to justify asking for time off to go to New York.

"Well, this is wonderful," said Jean-Marc after reading the first paragraph or so. "Congratulations! You know, if I can give you advice, you should really open up some more. You're obviously a talented guy, we all saw that with the design you did for the Network. It's your interpersonal skills that are lacking. I know the staff here tends to be quiet during the day, but you're on a whole other level compared to everyone else. That's going to set you back. Take my word for it."

"I know," I said. I told Jean-Marc that I was a "reserved person," which seemed easier than trying to explain to him my strategy of deliberately avoiding socializing with my co-workers as a way to avoid developing any kind of emotional connection to this job.

I left the newspaper on Jean-Marc's desk and then returned to my station. About half an hour later, Jean-Marc stormed out of his office.

"Excuse me, everyone," Jean-Marc said, addressing the room. "I have two public announcements I'd like to make. Let's start with the good stuff. So as you all know, I think it's important to celebrate our individual accomplishments just as much as our accomplishments as a team. In case you haven't heard, we have two rock stars in the office. Two! The first one is Fabio, whose music group outside the office has been booked for Ottawa Rock Explosion. Is that what it's called? The festival?"

"It's something like that," said Fabio.

"Anyway," said Jean-Marc. "You should all listen to Fabio's band. I love it! It's very groovy."

"Where can we do that?" said Anish.

"On Bandcamp," said Fabio. "We have demos on there. I play bass. It's rock music."

"The second rock star, he sits in the back and he doesn't talk much, but don't underestimate him," said Jean-Marc. "He's doing some pretty interesting things. It's Daniel."

Everyone turned around and looked at me. I waved a little, not knowing how else to react. No one waved back.

"This is an article about an art show that he did, I encourage all of you to read it," said Jean-Marc. "Daniel, the next time you show your work, you should tell us. We'll come see it. It can be a little office road trip."

"Sure," I said, hoping that day would never come.

"Now, I have another item on the agenda," said Jean-Marc. "I am going to arrange for a photographer to come in and take portraits of all of you. I've been thinking about how we can push authenticity so that when students visit the Network, they develop a more personal connection to the people behind the site. The new portraits are going to go on the company website, plus we're going to use them to open social media accounts for everyone that will automatically be linked to your Network profile."

"Shit," I thought. I wasn't sure how to tell Jean-Marc that I didn't want my name to be associated online with this job in any way, because it might destroy the illusion that I was succeeding as an independent artist.

30

"When do you get here?" typed Eloise on Facebook Chat. It was the second week of May and Jean-Marc had officially approved my time off to go to New York.

"Next Thursday," I typed. "I am taking the train with Jane in the morning."

"Nice," typed Eloise. "Is Grace coming with you? And do you both need a place to stay? Train is so fancy."

"Grace can't come," I typed. "She's saving her vacation days to go back to Newfoundland this summer, it's her dad's big work anniversary. And Jane will be staying with a friend of hers, but I still haven't found a place."

"Okay," said Eloise. "Well, I am subletting this room and staying at Rebecca's apartment half of the time, so either the couch at Rebecca's or my room will be empty at any given time. You can sleep there. You and Jane will be here so soon."

"I know," I typed. "I keep feeling like we should be there

already. Last night, you posted a picture on Instagram and I looked at it and it was almost like I was expecting to recognize myself in the background somewhere."

"The lineup for next week is ridiculously sensational," typed Eloise.

31

Some weeks I didn't floss because if I couldn't hurt myself anymore, what did I even have left.

32

Several days later, I sat next to Jane in the café car of a train on our way to New York, with our laptops forming a kind of makeshift wall. Glancing at her screen, I noticed that her hard drive was named "World Peace."

"So many notifications," Jane said, staring down at her phone. "Every app wants to be the most important thing in my life. What I really need is an app that tells all my other apps to fuck off."

"Do you want Adderall?" I said.

"Do you have some?" said Jane. "I would totally have some. Adderall is the best. It's like Gatorade for artists."

"Grace lets me have her leftovers, so I basically get free Adderall just as long as I don't go overboard," I said. "I don't think I could have survived March without Adderall."

"Can I show you something?" said Jane, opening a web browser. "I forgot to tell you this, but I am getting paid to make a video for NewHive. Do you know that site? I am nowhere near done, but I just want to give you an idea of what I am going for."

"Sure," I said.

"I've been meaning to do something on the topic of excessive waste for a while," said Jane. "I just couldn't figure out how to flesh out the concept until now. I got this idea from the little girl I babysit. She doesn't understand that groceries cost money, so she wastes a lot of food. I have to tell her, 'A cow made that milk for you, you're just going to throw that away?' I am trying to be careful and not brainwash her into becoming a vegetarian, but I am probably not doing a good job. I keep telling her that corporations are evil."

"It's something she'll have to learn eventually," I said. "Might as well teach her now."

"That's what I think, too," said Jane. "I want to add background music for the video as well, but Elliot is kind of mad at me right now, so I might have to ask someone else to do the soundtrack."

"Why?" I said.

"We had this talk a few days ago," said Jane. "I've been growing resentful of how boring stability is. I tried talking to him about opening our relationship so that we could date other people, but I am not sure he got it. It's not that I don't love him anymore or anything like that, it's just that I feel like I need to challenge myself to get into new situations more. When you're in a stable relationship, it's so easy to crawl back to safety and stay home with your lover and do nothing all the time, you know? I just want to find a better balance between safety and risk. Do you ever feel like that with Grace?"

"Sometimes," I said. "I keep telling myself that I am capable of committing to another person and having a stable, long-term relationship and stuff, but then I look at what I am doing and it's like, I can barely seem to commit to watching a movie online that's ninety minutes long. Sometimes I wonder if my love life is just going to end up being a succession of different relationships that last two to five years each, like contracts for baseball players. That seems more realistic to me than one big relationship where you get married and spend decades together."

"I have no idea how other people do this," said Jane, laughing. "I feel like Nietzsche right now. Monogamy is dead."

33

"We're in Manhattan being advertised to death," I told Eloise over text message.

34

The lobby at Blindside featured blue lighting, hand-painted leaves on the wall and old TV sets nested in an arrangement of fake and real plants. It was early afternoon and Jane and I were meeting with someone named Danielle, who ran the space, so that we could set up in preparation for the show. Up on a wall was a medium-sized poster advertising the exhibit, including the names of the nine artists on display, all women except me. *Pretend You're Not Here* was the title of the show. "Constant phone use encouraged," read a sentence at the bottom of the poster.

"I am so happy we came," said Jane about twenty minutes later while calibrating a projector. "I am not even sure what's happening right now."

"What do you mean?" I said.

"I mean, are we in Brooklyn?" said Jane. "How did we get here again? When did we make all this stuff? What's happening?"

"I don't know," I said, laughing. "You're right. Now that I think about it, I have no idea how any of this happened."

A few hours passed. Working alongside Jane, I found myself thinking about our friendship, tried to visualize what our future together would look like. Though I was used to friends coming in and out of my life, I could imagine Jane and I still being friends well into our forties, us becoming yuppie artists together maybe, exhibiting zany video art about our condos in a small gallery somewhere. I could see our lives growing in parallel, our respective romantic relationships falling apart every couple of years or so, forcing us to rely on one another for companionship and support instead, a sort of platonic, sideways relationship.

Jane and I left Blindside to go get food. By the time we got back, it was early evening and the gallery was already about a quarter full. Exploring the main room, I found myself mentally comparing the space I was in to the Facebook event that Eloise had created to advertise the show. It seemed strange to encounter an object of desire in real life, almost as if I wasn't sure how to interact with it without the screen between us.

Later, Eloise introduced Jane and I to different faces, describing us as "important artists" before adding, "like everyone else here" and laughing.

A face asked me how I made money for a living and I said, "I don't."

A face said insane things about Sol Lewitt and conceptual art and minimalism.

A face asked Jane, "So, when are you moving here?" assuming that Jane was planning to move to New York at some point like everyone else.

A face said that glitch art was played out and "a little too

217

ten years ago," not realizing that my piece was the one with glitches in it.

Watching Eloise socialize, I began to realize how much her reality had changed in the past year or so. I felt like I was no longer a central character in her life, but had become instead some sort of occasional guest star. It was only by coming here and witnessing her reality in person that I was finally able to understand why she had been so desperate to avoid moving back to Toronto.

A few hours later, several people complained about a loud, unpleasant man who was going around the room and making fun of the works on display, trying to impress the woman who was accompanying him. Eloise decided to confront him, inviting him to leave.

"Oh, so I can't critique the art?" the man said.

"Critiquing is fine, shitting on everything and deliberately being a dick isn't," said Eloise. "Let's see your fucking art. If you think this is easy, it's not."

"I never said that," said the man.

"I think you should leave," said Eloise.

"Excuse me, is this your gallery?" the man said. "Do you own this place? Because you can't ask me to leave for critiquing the art. This is ridiculous."

"Okay," said Eloise. "I am going to step outside now so that I don't strangle you with a power cord."

Eloise walked away. Jane and I followed her outside, joining the crowd standing on the sidewalk in front of the space.

"Can you believe that guy?" said Eloise. "Lord, what an asshole."

"I know," said Jane. "You looked like you were about to go on a warpath in there. You looked like you were about to transform into the Hulk."

"Has that ever happened in the comic books?" I said. "Bruce Banner turns into the Hulk because of a hater at one of his art shows?"

"I don't know," said Jane. "There should be a comic book where he turns into the Hulk because he's angry about systemic inequality or rape culture."

"Every time I think I am done arguing with art bros, they find a way to pull me back in," said Eloise. "It's like being part of a cult. I don't think I can ever leave."

"The art bro works in mysterious ways," I said.

"I wanted to look forward to tonight and saying goodbye to everyone, but I had this feeling that something bad was going to happen," said Eloise. "In a way, it seems so fitting that my time here would end with some man coming in and shitting on everything."

"Don't let one shithead ruin your night," said Jane. "It's just one guy."

"It's more than that," said Eloise. "I also feel bad that we couldn't pay anyone. I am so sick of being financially impotent. Why did we all do so much labour for free tonight? We're all adults. We all need money to live. This is nuts. What are we all doing with our lives?"

35

We moved to a bar nearby, then a rooftop party, then a public park where we sat in a botched circle and drank from an enormous, jug-like bottle of vodka that looked like a prop from a movie set, maybe a comedy titled *Honey, I Shrunk the Important Artists Who All Have Side-Jobs*. It was 3 a.m. We chatted for a while, then some people went home, then Eloise cried and Jane cried and someone else cried and I sat there mourning my ability to cry. Eloise, Jane and I all ended up falling asleep on the grass. A few hours later, I awoke and checked my phone for the time and realized that Jane and I would have to leave soon to catch our train back to Montreal. I spoke with Jane, and we both agreed that we didn't feel ready to leave just yet. I made a mental note to email Jean-Marc to notify him that I would be staying an extra day and felt confident that I wouldn't forget, even though I immediately did.

36

In the bathroom of a cheap breakfast restaurant, I noticed that someone had written, "Smash the patriarchy" in elegant pink glitter on a wall near the sink. I drank water from the tap and then looked at my face in the mirror, analyzing my reflection like I was searching for another face within the face. A few minutes later, I returned to our table and sat across from Eloise and Jane, who had ordered coffee.

"I don't know if I'll miss New York," said Eloise, "but I'll miss Blindside. My definition of 'home' has been pretty fluid in the past year, so that place felt like the closest thing I had to one."

"What are you going to do next?" said Jane.

"I am still not sure," said Eloise. "I need to make money, but it feels like robots have started to take all the normal jobs and all that's out there now is call centre or struggling artist. When I try to picture what's next, I think I imagine something completely different, like moving to a forest and logging off and changing my name to 'McDonalds' so that algorithms can't find me. That's going to be my big rebellion. Logging off. Fuck art and having to chase people all the time to get paid and purposefully making your life miserable. I think I am done. I hope global warming wipes out the entire fucking internet."

"That seems strangely hopeful to me," I said. "It sounds almost like what I've been getting out of Zen Buddhism. It tells you something completely different. It tells you to become nothing."

37

When I am dead, take my ashes and make a computer with them.

38

I awoke to a text message from Grace telling me that Jean-Marc, who was expecting me to come in to work that morning, had called her asking about my absence. "Shit, I completely forgot to email him," I thought. Opening my laptop, I quickly composed an electronic message addressed to Jean-Marc, telling him that I had been "delayed." Waiting for his response, I refreshed Facebook and saw that the website Dazed Digital had published a short, unremarkable but also largely positive blog post about our show. The best parts of the article were the high-res photographs, plus a quote from Eloise. "Internet art in general is shallow, overrated and probably redundant at this point," the quote read, "so I am not interested in internet art that's gimmicky, which is just as interesting to me as phone art or fax art. The artists we're presenting all use the internet and digital life as part of their practice in some way, but calling it 'internet art' is sort of missing the point. It's more like, they speak from a personal perspective, and that perspective just happens to include the internet."

A few minutes later, I received an email from Jean-Marc simply asking me to come see him the next day.

39

At the Canadian border, Jane and I stood in line, waiting for our turn. The guard processing Jane, who seemed bored, made a comment about her headphones, mentioning that he owned a pair of the same brand.

"Those are professional DJ headphones," said Jane. "Are you a professional DJ on the side?"

The guard looked flustered, as if suddenly realizing he shouldn't have shared personal information with us.

"If I was, I wouldn't tell you," he said, trying to regain his composure.

"That guy was totally a DJ on the side," said Jane about twenty minutes later.

"We should google him to see if we can find his Soundcloud," I said.

"DJ Anything to Declare," said Jane, laughing.

40

"Let me get this right," said Jean-Marc, lecturing me about my absence, though sounding more hurt than upset. It was a day later and I was sitting on a chair in his office. "On Sunday, you already knew that you wouldn't be back on time, but you didn't think of warning me right away? I had to call your wife?"

"I figured you wouldn't check your inbox until Monday

morning, so I thought I could email you on Sunday night," I said, "but then I forgot."

"You forgot," said Jean-Marc. "That's your excuse? How old are you again?"

"I am 30," I said.

"You're 30," said Jean-Marc. "And you don't have the common sense to warn me as soon as possible that you're going to be missing a day of work?"

"You're right," I said. "I should have warned you sooner. It's my fault. I apologize if my absence yesterday caused problems here."

"Of course it's your fault!" said Jean-Marc. "I don't know anyone else whose fault it could be. It's certainly not mine! Look, if you have other things going on in your life and you don't want to be here, then don't be here. If you're here, you need to be a professional. I don't think you fully understand that we're a growing company. If the Network takes off, I am going to have to hire at least four or five new people before the end of the year."

"I am sorry, but I don't think the Network is going to take off," I said. "I really feel like someone should tell you that. If I am honest, I just can't realistically conceive of a student who would find that website interesting."

"Well, that's why we got you to redesign it," said Jean-Marc. "Pushing authenticity is also going to help."

"That's another thing," I said. "I don't want to open social media accounts that link my name to this company. The best I can do is use a pseudonym."

"That's doesn't work for me," said Jean-Marc. "I need authenticity. Look, I can see that you're talented and that you bring a unique skillset to the team, which is why I am being lenient with you, but I need a commitment here. I can guarantee you it's going to pay off. I have big plans. The staff that's in place now, in five years, you could all be managing departments. Don't you want that?"

"No," I said.

41

I told Grace that I had essentially fired myself and she seemed neither thrilled nor surprised.

42

Only interesting things would happen if "art" was suddenly renamed "rap metal."

43

At a grocery store in Outremont, Grace and I ran into Roberto, who was buying chocolate soy milk. I asked Roberto how married life was treating him and he said that everything was good, although getting his permanent residency status was complicated and already causing some problems between Ashlyn and him. They shared a bank account because he couldn't legally open his own and had had to hire a lawyer to facilitate his citizenship application. Roberto had been asked to provide a large number of documents that were all difficult to procure, including an official certificate from the Mexican government stating that he had completed his military service. Back in Mexico, he explained, military service was mandatory, though he had been discharged after only a summer of basic training. Listening to Roberto, I imagined him wearing a camo outfit, being yelled at by an army sergeant during a drill, then laughing nervously, hoping to avoid a conflict with his sergeant.

As we said goodbye, I tried to visualize the sheer amount of bureaucracy that Roberto would have to endure over the next year or so in order to get his permanent residency status. It seemed insane how most of my efforts in life went towards trying not to have a job, while most of Roberto's efforts in life went towards simply being able to have one.

44

On the first Friday of June, Grace flew to Newfoundland to attend a formal ceremony in honour of her's dad's thirty-year work anniversary. A day later, I realized she had taken her Adderall supply with her, forcing me to take a break from the drug. In the days that followed, I looked for freelancing work in a sluggish and unmotivated manner, experienced the effects of withdrawal, grew depressed a little. "Adderall crash," I thought. "Unemployed without borders," I thought. I watched Tom-Tom paw a plastic mouse with little conviction or enthusiasm, something that seemed less like genuine cat behaviour to me, and more like his imitation of a cat, a kind of satire. Eventually, I was able to find work, though not the type I had been looking for. In exchange for money, I agreed to take care of a pug for a few weeks for an artist in his early forties who I had met at an opening once.

Having the apartment to myself felt like a preview of what life without Grace could be like. Living alone with an apartment-sized dog seemed like a lifestyle for which I was perfectly suited, what I had always assumed my life would one day turn into, like the final evolution of a Pokémon. Walking the pug around my neighbourhood every day, I found myself noticing how strangers would smile at me more, how other dog owners would nod at me, like we were part of some sort of secret brother-hood.

"Living alone with a dog," I thought.

"This is 40," I thought.

The cats disliked the pug, but were mostly ignoring him, as if pretending he didn't exist. Tom-Tom was more concerned with Grace's absence than with the pug's presence. Every morning, he would jump on our bed expecting to see Grace, only to discover that her side of the mattress was still unoccupied.

"Wow, you look so lonely," I said one morning, petting Tom-Tom's head. "I hadn't realized how much you love Grace."

A few hours later, I found him sleeping on one of her work shirts.

45

Felt incredibly bored with myself, almost like I was waiting for myself to leave so that I could finally be alone.

46

Why wasn't my life making me money again? It seemed like I was always working, was always producing content, except my content usually profited large platforms like Facebook or Twitter instead of me. My economic life felt like a kind of real-time experiment in which I was always looking for the next hustle, was rarely able to earn money for work I had completed in the past. I couldn't afford to pay for everything I downloaded so I didn't, which sounded good on paper, except it meant that somewhere down the road, a band would only be able to afford to give me $80 in exchange for creating a muisc video for them. In that way, maybe my pirating-heavy lifestyle was making me poorer, not richer. I could try to get a depressing office job in order to afford being an artist, but that might only be a short-term fix considering that more and more jobs would become automated in the next twenty years or so. Would I be able to fall back on a depressing office job then? Would they even exist anymore? And if Facebook was going to spy on me, steal my data, benefit from my content and generate absurd profits, why couldn't I profit in some way from that? If we don't pay people properly for the content they create, how else were we going to earn money in the future when all the sad ofice jobs are gone?

47

I received a text message from Grace, who wanted to let me know that her flight had just landed at the Montreal airport. "Would you mind going to Andrea's place and picking up emergency weed for me?" a second text message said. "I completely ran out. I was in Blaze Mode while I was home, so I just burned through my stash."

"No problem," I wrote back. "Just tell Andrea I'll stop by in about half an hour."

"Thank you so much," Grace replied. "My Nan says hi, by the way. She kept saying, 'Tells Daniel we loves him.' It was cute."

I cleaned the apartment a little, then headed over to Andrea's place. We made small talk in her doorway for a bit and she asked me a few questions about New York.

"Look at you," said Andrea. "There's an article about you on *Dazed*, you travel to New York for a show. You seem so successful lately."

"Yeah," I said, and then immediately thought, "My main source of income right now is dog-sitting for money."

When I got back to the apartment, I saw that Grace had returned home. She was playing with the pug, looked calm and re-energized.

"Oh my god, he's so goofy-looking," said Grace, smiling. "I love how his tongue sticks out to the left."

"Yeah, it's actually been really nice having him around," I said. "Maybe that's what I should do full-time. Dog-sit for money."

"Do you really want to do that full-time?" said Grace. "I am not trying to make fun of you, I just think it's funny."

"At this point, I mean, why not?" I said. "I just don't think I can have an office job anymore. It feels like the opposite of being alive. At least with dog-sitting, I get exercise and I feel like I am making a concrete difference in some dog's life."

"That sounds fine," said Grace, "though to be honest, I feel like you might end up quitting out of nowhere because you want to go to New York again or something."

"I am sorry I am impossible with jobs," I said. "I need flexibility, so it's hard to make something work for more than a couple of months."

"I don't mind that you're passionate about your work," said Grace. "You know me, I am always down for smoking weed and watching *MasterChef*, so I find your work ethic motivating. The problem with you is that wanting to be productive leads you to being self-destructive."

"You think I am self-destructive?" I said.

I don't know," said Grace. "Self-destructive might be harsh, but you don't seem too far off from that."

"I just value my time," I said.

"And that's fine, except sometimes it seems like all you care about is trying to be productive," said Grace. "I feel like I have to hold your hand into wanting to do anything else. Maybe that's why you're good at saving money. You just tune out reality a lot."

"Maybe, but then that's why you're good for me," I said.

"You say that," said Grace, "but when I ask you to go out for food or something, I just know you're automatically thinking, 'Shit, I am going to have to spend money.'"

"Well, you know I don't care about food all that much, so going out for food just feels like a waste of money to me," I said. "I go along with it mostly because I like seeing you happy, but it always feels like there's a part of me that's just sitting there resenting my dumb expensive restaurant food. I don't know why you want me to go with you when you know it's only fun for you. I can't help feeling like that's selfish of you."

"Well, sorry for wanting to enjoy my fucking life, Daniel," said Grace.

"It's not that I don't want you to enjoy your life, it's that you automatically assume that food equals happiness without caring whether or not that's also true for me," I said. "Can't you see how that's fucked up?"

"No, I don't see how that's fucked up," said Grace. "Calling it 'fucked up' is what's fucked up. It's a restaurant. Eat the fucking food and feel good. That's it. It's not a fucking physics class."

"I don't know," I said. "I disagree."

"You disagree about what?" said Grace. "You know, sometimes I wonder if we even have things in common or if we're just two people who met at a loft party."

"We wouldn't have dated this long if we had nothing in common," I said.

"The frustrating thing with you is that you have great qualities, like if you just tried, I could see you becoming a good dad," said Grace.

"Can I ask you something?" I said. "Why do you even want to have children at all? Being a woman doesn't have to mean becoming a mother, the same way not everyone who makes art should live in New York."

"Why do I think I want to have a kid?" said Grace. "Because I think I'd be a good mom and because I think I want to know what that's like. It doesn't have to be more complicated than that."

"I don't think that's why you want to have a kid," I said. "I think you're desperate to prove to your dad that maybe you're not a fuck-up after all and that you managed to get your shit together. It's like your pointless revenge on your dad for making you feel like you were a disappointment to him."

Grace wanted to say something, but began tearing up.

"I am sorry, I am not trying to be mean," I said. "I just don't understand how you can get excited about having children when we keep watching documentaries telling us that we have too many humans already and that the planet is fucked. It's, like, impossible to be optimistic. Plus, having a kid is so insanely expensive. How do you even afford it?"

"I don't know if this is working anymore," said Grace.

48

Jane asked me if I wanted anything from the convenience store and I thought, "Do I want anything?"

49

Maybe my real problem with having children wasn't climate trauma or my inability to see myself ever being financially stable, but simply that having kids would mean having to give up being able to be alone.

50

In a book about Zen Buddhism, I stumbled on another anecdote about the Original Face. "'What was your original face before you were born, before your parents were born?' the man asked the woman," the passage read. "She answered his question by sitting in silence for a moment with her eyes closed, then simply added, 'Do you understand?'"

51

My own future laughed at me.

ESPLANADE
Books

THE FICTION IMPRINT AT VÉHICULE PRESS